The Trails Are as Scenic as the Place

The Parkers slowed their car as they drove through busy Bar Harbor, Maine, in the mid-afternoon. The sidewalks were filled with tourists walking along and shopping. Once they were beyond the quaint town, they entered Acadia National Park in the forested Sieur de Monts section. Morgan, James, Mom, and Dad got out of the car and walked over to a sign that read WILD GARDENS OF ACADIA.

The family strolled through the lush and manicured botanical preserve. They learned of Acadia's fauna and the areas of the park they were found in: mixed woods, mountains, meadow, seaside, thicket, marsh, and pond, among others.

Standing in the shade of a white birch surrounded by ferns, Dad said, "It's a little paradise in here."

The Parkers meandered over to the pond habitat area. There they settled on the wooden footbridge and examined the lily pads, ferns, and plants of the mini-terrain.

James lay down and peered into the water. "Hey! There are pollywogs in there!"

"And look," Morgan pointed. "There's a frog on a leaf."

The Parkers watched the amphibians. While the pollywogs glided from one spot to another, the frog lay on the surface perfectly still.

"There's another one over here," Dad whispered. Morgan snapped a photo then said, "They're so still, they almost look fake." As if hearing her comment, the frog plopped into the water, showing how real it was.

After a few more minutes in the gardens, the family visited the nature center nearby that was filled with information about the wildlife of Acadia. The Parkers meandered among the displays, then went to the ranger's desk. They wanted to get in a little hike after the long drive and before settling into camp.

The ranger showed the family a map and suggested the Emery-Homans loop trail that started right behind the visitor center.

"It's just a mile, then we'll head to our campsite at Blackwoods," Mom said to her family as they walked out the door. So the Parkers jaunted over to the Homans Trail and began hiking.

Instantly the path led the Parkers up a series of carved granite stairs. After several minutes of climbing, Dad said, "Well, this is a nice little workout after all of our plane and car travel getting here."

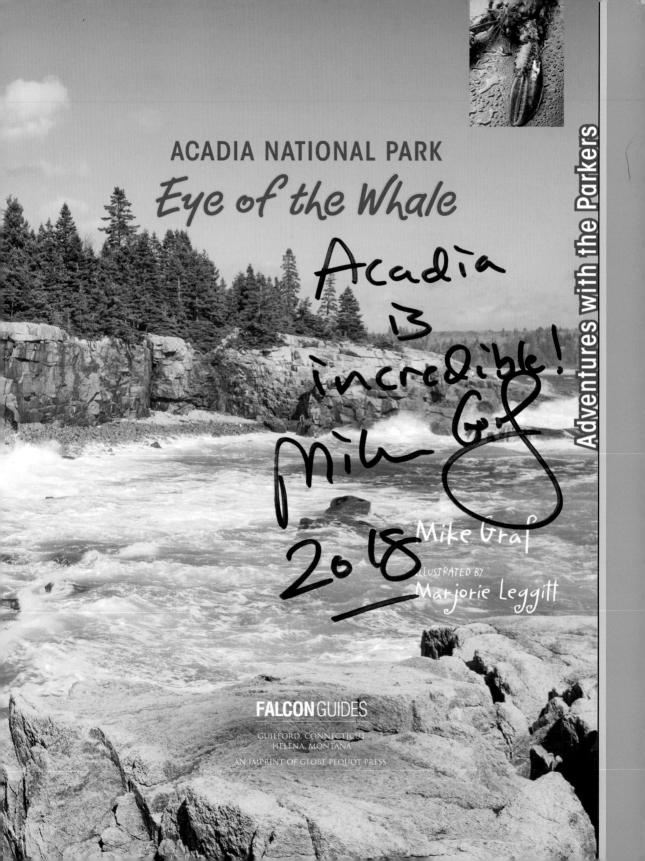

ACADIA NATIONAL PARK
Eye of the Whale

Mike Graf

ILLUSTRATED BY
Marjorie Leggitt

FALCONGUIDES

GUILFORD, CONNECTICUT
HELENA, MONTANA
AN IMPRINT OF GLOBE PEQUOT PRESS

(handwritten inscription) Acadia is incredible! Mike Graf 2018

FALCONGUIDES®

Text © 2013 Mike Graf
Illustrations © 2013 Marjorie Leggitt

FalconGuides is an imprint of Globe Pequot Press.
Falcon, FalconGuides, and Outfit Your Mind are registered trademarks of Morris Book Publishing, LLC.

Illustrations: Marjorie Leggitt
Models for twins: Amanda and Ben Frazier

Photos by Mike Graf and Kimberly Alexander Graf with the following exceptions: p. 5 Paul Marshall; and the following, which are licensed by Shutterstock.com: inside front cover/p. i © Tim Kornoelje; p. i inset © picturepartners; p. 7 © Colin D. Young; pp. 9, 44 © Jeffrey M. Frank; pp. 29, 31 © T. Markley; p. 37 © Zack Frank; p. 38 top © dp photography; p. 38 bottom © kurdistan; p. 41 © Jerry Whaley; p. 45 © Celeste Costa Photography; pp. 72, 94/insideback cover © Lynda Lehmann; p. 75 © David Ashley; p. 81 © jaytee; p. 82 © Brett Atkins; p. 85 © spirit of america; p. 86 © David Kay; p. 88 © Tom Reichner; p. 92 © Stephen

Map courtesy of National Park Service

Project editor: Julie Marsh
Layout: Melissa Evarts

Library of Congress Cataloging-in-Publication Data

Graf, Mike.
Acadia National Park : eye of the whale / Mike Graf ; illustrated by Marjorie Leggitt.
    pages cm. — (Adventures with the Parkers)
 ISBN 978-0-7627-8262-8
1. Acadia National Park (Me.)—Guidebooks—Juvenile literature. I. Leggitt, Marjorie C., illustrator. II. Title.
 F27.M9G7 2013
 974.1'45—dc23
                                                              2013003352

Printed in the United States of America
10 9 8 7 6 5 4 3 2 1

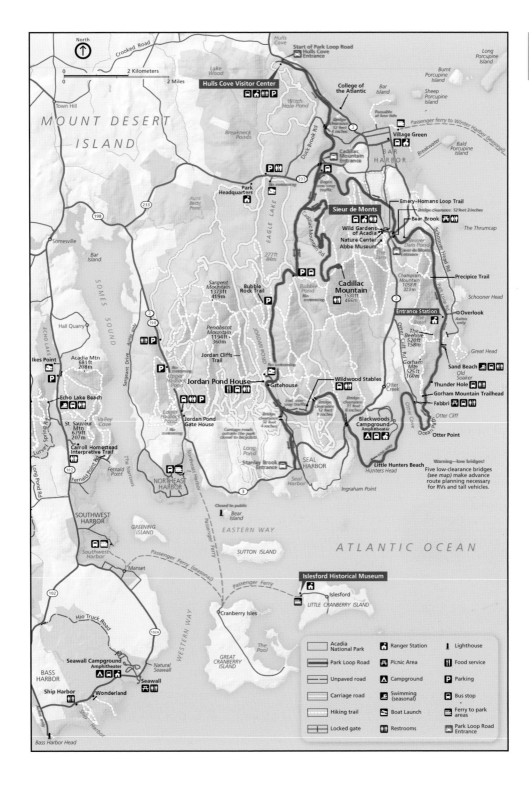

They kept on climbing up the steep and seemingly never-ending stone steps. "This is quite a trail," James mentioned about halfway up.

Eventually the pathway leveled off. There the Parkers took in distant ocean and island views and gazed far below at the mostly forested Sieur de Monts area and the marshy Great Meadow.

The family continued skirting along the flatter plateau and then began the long descent on the Emery Path.

"What goes up must come down," Morgan said while carefully negotiating the steep stairs down.

"I don't know about all of you," Dad said, "but this trail sure whets my appetite for more."

Finally the Parkers returned to level ground and their car. They drove a short distance to Blackwoods Campground. After checking in, they found their assigned site #93. They set up camp, ate a quick dinner, and hustled over to the amphitheater for the evening program.

The talk had already started by the time the Parkers arrived, so they sat in the back. The ranger, Angie, was scrolling through pictures of Acadia's trails and asking the audience to guess where they were.

At a picture of a small lake, someone in the audience called out, "The Bowl!"

"Right you are," Angie replied.

On a mountaintop, someone shouted, "Cadillac Mountain!"

"Boy, we sure have some hikers in the audience," Angie said.

In a forested region with a peek of the ocean, a person correctly guessed, "Wonderland?"

On a steep ascent with iron rungs and ladders for climbing, another person called out, "The Precipice!"

"Yep," Angie replied. "And it's probably the most challenging and talked about of all our hikes here in the park."

Then Angie flipped to a trail showing a bunch of hikers scaling a rocky dome high above the ground.

"The Beehive," several voices called.

Next Angie displayed a gentle trail near the ocean with lots of people strolling along it.

"The Ocean Path" was the answer, to which Angie replied, "Not all of our trails have steep, rocky ascents, but they are all beautiful!"

Finally, after several more trail photos, a picture came up of steep granite stairs with a small rock bridge overhanging them.

"The Emery-Homans Loop Trail!" James exclaimed.

"Exactly!" Angie said. "And one of our most historic trails."

The Parkers smiled at each other, knowing they had already hiked a great trail and there were many more to come.

Angie told the crowd about Acadia's trails. "They are one of the most famous things about the park. A man named Waldron Bates was a pioneer trail builder here at Acadia in the early 1900s. You can see his classically constructed cairns all over the park."

Angie switched slides to show several of the Bates-styled cairns along Acadia's trails.

"Later George Dorr, often called the Father of Acadia, continued implementing granite carved pathways among our trails. In the 1930s the Civilian Conservation Corps, or CCC, also built many of our paths."

Bates cairn

Angie went on showing historical and modern pictures of Acadia's trails.

"The goal here," Angie said, "has always been that the trail is as important as the destination, and it should be just as beautiful as the landscape itself."

Mom leaned toward her family and whispered, "Just like the one we were on."

"Today," Angie built to her conclusion, "the organization Friends of Acadia is funding work on maintaining, restoring, and even opening new trails for our park. So, please," she concluded, "take a hike here in Acadia somewhere, if you can."

The audience clapped and then Angie invited everyone to come up front and see samples of carved-granite steps as well as the tools used to craft them.

While watching Angie demonstrate some of the stonemasonry involved in carving granite, Dad mentioned to his family, "That's a lot of work!"

Then Morgan said, "I know what we're going to be doing a lot of the next two weeks!"

"Hiking!" the clan chimed in.

Do You Think We Look Like Bees Up Here?

Morgan, James, Mom, and Dad started hiking on the forested, but also rocky, Beehive Trail.

At a clearing, the family got a glimpse of the granite dome that awaited them. "Are we *really* doing that?" James said, noticing a few hikers carefully skirting a precarious ledge far above.

Mom quickly tried to divert the nerves by changing the subject. "I read that the granite here in Acadia originated over four hundred million years ago as part of an ancient volcano."

"So that's what we'll be hiking on?" Morgan said.

Soon the family got another view of the trail that loomed above. "Wow!" Dad gasped, nervously but with excitement.

A woman coming down the trail approached the family. "Did you just hike *down* that?" Dad asked.

"No," the woman replied. "I'm just reminiscing. I've already hiked the Beehive once in my life, and I think that's enough."

As the woman walked on, Morgan and James each thought to themselves, *what if the trail is too much for us?*

Mom also wondered aloud. "You know, we can always turn around at the base of the climbing part. We don't have to do this."

Soon they came to a warning sign: CAUTION: EXPOSED CLIFFS AND IRON RUNGS WITH STEEP DROP-OFFS. NOT FOR THOSE WITH FEAR OF HEIGHTS.

Dad looked at his apprehensive family. "Are we all good?"

James nodded and then said, "At least for now."

Soon the Parkers arrived at the first of a series of climbs up the massive rock. At one point James saw people watching them from below. "Look!" he called out with a sense of pride from where he already was. "They're waving!"

James and Morgan waved back.

Mom asked, "So far, so good, right? Are you all for going on?"

Morgan and James nodded their heads, "Yes."

"Personally," Dad said, "I'm loving this, but we're also at the point of no return. It's easier to hike up these iron rungs and ledges than to hike down."

The Parkers caught up to another group. They slithered to the side and let Morgan, James, Mom, and Dad go by. "We're far too slow," one of them said. Then she turned to her friends and asked, "Are you sure you want to hike the Precipice Trail next?"

The mention of the Precipice again planted a seed in the Parkers' minds, and as they continued up the Beehive, their confidence grew with each passing obstacle.

Mom took the lead now and coached, "Hold onto that tree there. It's a good grip as we cross here."

On another precarious point, Mom said to the twins, "I've got a good hold right here. And I'm not going anywhere if you need to grab onto my hand."

The Parkers followed Mom's cues and climbed on, slowly and steadily. On a long, exposed section, Dad went first. "Let's go one at a time here. Hold onto the bar along the way, OK?"

One by one, Morgan, James, and finally Mom followed. Once they were all across the narrow, exposed ledge, Dad said, "This really is just like rock climbing without being roped up."

At another narrow ledge with steep drop-offs, the Parkers stayed as far as they could from the edge and rested a moment. "There are more people waving at us," Morgan said. "I wonder if we really do look like bees buzzing around a hive up here."

A moment later, Mom asked, "Are we all ready to go on?"

"Yes" was the quick reply.

Mom now led through a catwalk-like section with bars for holding onto on both sides. "It's a little tricky in here," she guided.

A few more climbs and handholds later, and the cliff gave way to sloping rock. Dad looked up, noticing the cairn trail markers leading up the rest of the way. "I think we've made it through the toughest part!" he announced. "Congratulations are in order!" Dad high-fived Morgan, James, and Mom, toasting their achievement.

Soon the trail topped off and began a short descent down to a body of water called the Bowl. The now deeply forested pathway led directly to a rocky area next to the large pond. Several people were nearby, dipping their feet into the water on a rare hot day in Acadia.

Dad wiped the sweat off his brow. "I know what I'm going to do! Anyone care to join me?"

Dad took off his shoes, and Morgan, James, and Mom did the same. Then all four Parkers plunged in and started splashing each other. It was quite a celebration. Once soaked, they climbed out and sat on the rocks to dry off.

"There," James said. "We've now graduated to the next level. Do you think the Precipice is waiting for us?"

Mom smiled. "Let's enjoy this accomplishment first. We can consider that one later!"

The family pulled out snacks and ate silently while enjoying the well-earned scenery.

Morgan's New Friend

The Parkers stepped onto the boat and took a seat. As the *Sea Princess* chugged out of the harbor, Dad noticed the blue skies dotted with white, puffy clouds and the calm seas. "It's a great day for a little cruise," he said to his family.

Once the boat was out of Northeast Harbor, the ranger on board stepped up.

"Welcome to the Islesford Cruise," she said. "I'm park ranger Wanda, and I'll be taking you out along our splendid waterways and eventually to Little Cranberry Island."

Mom looked over the wildlife identification chart given to each person. "Wow! Check out all these birds and sea mammals," she commented. "It looks like we may get to see a lot!"

The boat passed by Bear Island, and as it did, Wanda called out, "There's a cormorant right at three o'clock."

The passengers looked where the ranger pointed. The grayish white bird was perched on the rocky shore. "As you can see, cormorants are slim and have especially long necks. They're most famous for diving up to one hundred feet deep in water just to catch fish," Wanda described.

"Whoa!" Morgan said. "I think I can dive up to five feet deep."

The boat passed by colorful buoys spread throughout the water. Wanda explained, "Those buoys are all attached to lobster traps at the bottom of the ocean. Lobster, of course, is pretty famous here in Maine. Each person has a different-color pattern on their buoy so they can find it quickly and easily. The traps have a net in them with a hole designed so that a lobster can easily get in but it is very hard for them to get out. Fish and fish guts are the preferred bait for the traps, with herring being the most popular option."

The Parkers gazed out at all the buoys, each imagining what color pattern they would choose, if being a lobsterman was their job.

Wanda continued, "Traps have to be checked every two or three days. If there are lobsters in there and they have eaten all the bait, they'll eat each other!"

"I don't know if I'd like that job or not," James said, picturing the smell and gore involved.

Soon they approached Sutton Island. Wanda pointed out a large, branch-filled nest perched on some rocks just above the tidal zone. "A perfect spot for an osprey," she mentioned. "They eat fish, so it couldn't be in a better location."

Morgan snapped several pictures of the enormous nest.

"That nest has been used by multiple generations of osprey for over fifty years," Wanda said. "And a recent nesting pair was banded so we could monitor them. In winter they left the island. The female spent her winters in Haiti. The male decided the Miami area suited him just fine. But they returned every year in April within a week of each other."

"So interesting, huh?" Mom said to the family.

Someone at the other side of the boat called out, "Bald eagle—nine o'clock!"

Everyone excitedly shifted their gaze. The eagle was on top of a tree on Sutton Island, with its distinctive white head clearly showing.

"Our national symbol," Wanda said, "and an adult, too. Younger ones don't have the white heads yet."

The boat continued to cruise along, and the Parkers looked at the water and island scenery. They also gazed west to Mount Desert Island.

"It does look a little barren or deserted," Dad said. "At least those glacier-sculpted granite domes of rock seem to indicate the name of the island."

"You can definitely see the U-shape between the mountain bulges," Mom added. "Sure signs of glaciation. I read that glaciers were once up to two miles thick here."

Wanda gave more information about the area. "The water along coastal Maine is from a cold Canadian current. But cold water holds more oxygen, making our coastal waters a very rich habitat. Our ocean creatures love the cold water."

James leaned over toward his parents. "That's why we are going to go swimming at Echo Lake and not Sand Beach, right?"

"We'll try both," Mom replied. "But I have a feeling where we'll spend more time in the water."

"Speaking of ocean creatures," Wanda said, "everyone look at three o'clock."

"It's a seal!" Morgan called out.

"There are more over there," James added.

The passengers watched the seals in the water and on the rocks at East Bunker Ledge.

Morgan waved and called, "Hi, seal!" Then she looked at her family. "It's looking right at us!"

"Their faces look like puppy dogs," Mom said.

Wanda heard Mom. "Those are harbor seals. And many people describe them just like you did. They grow four to six feet long and weigh two hundred to three hundred pounds when fully grown. We often see them above the water, including that baby over there," Wanda pointed. "But they can actually dive and stay underwater for up to fifteen minutes."

James did some quick counting. "There are at least twenty of them out there."

While everyone on board watched and photographed the seals, Morgan looked around. She saw a fin protrude above the water, but it was gone in a split second. What was that? Morgan said to herself, hoping she would get a better look.

The animal reappeared. Its back arched above the water's surface, then it dipped back under, all in about a second's time. On the animal's third trip above water, a small baby was paralleling it, just a few feet away. This time Morgan noticed the adult's blunt-shaped nose.

Morgan's heart raced. She quickly estimated the location of where the animals would next appear from where she last saw them, and hoped they would surface again.

The mother and baby cooperated. Then Morgan glanced at the animal identification chart and called out, "Harbor porpoise, everyone! Nine o'clock!" The marine mammals both simultaneously rose above the water's surface and glided back under.

"So graceful," Mom commented to her daughter while Morgan tried to snap pictures.

"Good eyes, Morgan," Dad said.

Soon the boat had moved beyond the range of the two porpoises, and they were out of sight.

"Quite some nice surprises we're getting on our boat cruise today," Mom said, beaming.

"That was a treat," Wanda said, overhearing Mom again. "Porpoises are actually part of the whale family, and they grow up to six feet long. They can dive all the way to six hundred feet or more below the surface, but they usually stay near the top of the water to come up and breathe every twenty-five seconds or so. They are fairly common here in the Gulf of Maine."

Soon the boat slowed down, preparing to dock at Little Cranberry Island. "We have thirty minutes to walk around on Little Cranberry," Wanda told the visitors. "The park service has a very nice museum right off this dock, and there are shops and stores here and farther in town. But there are also streets just to wander around on, so there's plenty to do for all. And, sometimes," Wanda emphasized while looking right at Morgan and James,

Little Cranberry Island Museum

"some of the kids in town have prepared baked goods to sell to us, too. Enjoy, everyone, and see you here in thirty minutes back on the boat."

Morgan, James, Mom, and Dad walked off the boat. Right away, several shops grabbed their attention and they peeked in, keeping a thought on the time. They also took a quick look at the museum. Ship models, tools, photographs, and other objects such as clocks and harpoons from earlier days on the island led Mom to say, "I wish we had a few hours here, at least!"

Wanting to try to see more of the island, the family walked the relaxed streets of the little village, passing by island homes and several areas of stacked lobster traps. Morgan noticed three girls selling something at a makeshift stand in front of one of the houses next to the road.

While James, Dad, and Mom went to inspect the lobster traps, Morgan walked over to the girls. One was older, Morgan guessed near her babysitter's age, about sixteen.

Another was clearly younger, *probably in kindergarten or first grade,* Morgan thought. She wondered what the school was like on the island, or even if there was one.

The third girl looked nine or ten, exactly Morgan's age. Morgan walked up to them. "Hi," she said. "What are you selling?"

"Cookies," the girl Morgan's age answered. "We have chocolate chip, oatmeal raisin, and also some gingerbread." She pointed out each.

"You have just what I like!" Morgan smiled. She selected four of the treats and reached for her change purse while glancing back to see the rest of her family, now looking at a house with some ornamental garden displays.

"That will be four dollars," the girl said. "By the way, what's your name?"

"Morgan. What's yours?"

"Kaitlyn. Where are you from?"

Morgan paused for a second, picturing a map of the United States and how very far away her home was compared to where she was now. "San Luis Obispo, California. That's completely on the other side of the country, right near the Pacific Ocean." Morgan looked back toward the water. "The ocean there is pretty cold, too. We only go in during the summer. But even then, it's pretty chilly. My parents have wet suits."

Kaitlyn smiled. "I know where you live! Last summer my family and I went to California to go to Disneyland. But we also traveled to San Francisco, going up the coast. We stopped at Hearst's Castle. You live near there, right? Then we went to Lake Tahoe and Yosemite and saw the huge sequoia trees."

"Yes!" Morgan exclaimed. "You sure know a lot about California. By the way, I'm going into fifth grade next year. How about you?"

"Me too!" Kaitlyn beamed.

Morgan looked at the tiny island-bound village and compared it to her hometown. "Where do you go to school?"

"Right here on the island," Kaitlyn answered. "At the Ashley Bryan School. Last year there were ten students in the whole school. It's pretty cool."

"Ten students?" Morgan replied. "I had twenty-eight students in my fourth-grade class last year!"

"Wow," Kaitlyn said, picturing a very crowded, noisy classroom full of kids.

Morgan noticed James, Mom, and Dad approaching her. She remembered the limited time they had on the island and thought quickly. "I have to go in a second, but do you think I could write you? We could be pen pals!"

Kaitlyn beamed. "I would love that!"

The girls quickly jotted down addresses for each other. Morgan added on her note her family's e-mail address. "Do you get e-mail out here?"

"Of course," Kaitlyn replied. "But it isn't always reliable."

The rest of Morgan's family waltzed up. Morgan said to James, Mom, and Dad, "This is my new friend, Kaitlyn." She looked at James. "Can you take a picture of us?"

James took the camera and snapped a photo of his sister and Kaitlyn.

As the Parkers quickly headed for the boat, Morgan turned and called back, "I'll e-mail you the picture, OK?"

"I can't wait to see it! And I'll write back right away. I promise!"

The Parkers were the last to get on board. Once they sat down, Morgan took out the treats and shared them with her family.

They headed back to sea and eventually Mount Desert Island. On the way, Morgan mentioned, "I like Little Cranberry Island. I could see living there."

Mom smiled. "Us too, dear. Us too."

This Thing Probably Hates Me Right about Now

The next morning, Morgan, James, Mom, and Dad took the Island Explorer bus from their campground to the Otter Point parking lot. There they met rangers Nancy and Michael for Tidepool School. The rangers introduced themselves, then gave each child a nametag written on duct tape.

The two rangers, a dozen or so kids, and their parents crossed the highway. They walked along the Ocean Path to a short spur trail to a rocky tide pool zone near the sea.

There the rangers gathered everyone around a rocky bowl they called the Amphitheater. The rangers then went on to explain the cause of the tides.

After, Michael asked, "So, given what you know, what tidal stage do you think we are at now?"

"Low tide," James, Morgan, and several other children called out in unison.

"That's right," Ranger Michael said. "And it's the best time for exploring these tide pools."

The highest tides in the world occur just north of Acadia at the northeast end of the Gulf of Maine at the Bay of Fundy. This is mostly in Canada, but partially touches the state of Maine. There, tidal surges, or high tides, can get to fifty feet or more!

Tides are caused by gravity interacting between the earth and the moon. The gravitational attraction of the moon causes the oceans to bulge out in the moon's direction. Another, smaller bulge happens on the opposite side of the earth. Since the earth rotates every twenty-four hours, there are two high tides and two low tides daily.

Michael continued, "Because of Maine's rocky cliffs, the incoming tide has little place to spread out. So the tidal surge here is from eight to fourteen feet. That is about twice my height and one of the largest high tides in the world!"

The other ranger, Nancy, stepped up and asked for several volunteers. She took them to the side and gave each an object to hold behind their back until the right moment. "The tidal creatures we are about to find are what I call 'expert adapters,'" she said. "They have to be ready for all kinds of conditions," Nancy looked at the kids up front. "And our friends up here are going to show us what some of the elements are."

The first child in the group held up a bottle of moisturizer. "That's right," Nancy said. "With the water here coming and going, tidal creatures have to adapt and find ways to keep moist, such as staying under seaweed."

The next child in line held up a bottle of superglue. Nancy explained, "Yes, the waves do batter our tidal friends constantly. How do they deal with it? Some of them have their own type of glue and they cement themselves to the rocks. Pretty cool, huh?"

Morgan was next in line, and she held up a small container of sea salt. "The water is certainly salty around here," Nancy said. "You wouldn't want to drink it, that's for sure. But how salty it is depends on where the water is, how much rain has fallen in the pool, and how much evaporation has occurred. Our tidal friends are able to adapt to the various salt conditions."

Finally James showed the group a thermometer. "The temperature varies in these pools," Nancy said, "and our ocean friends have found ways to deal with that as well, some by hiding out in cooler areas such as under rocks."

Nancy looked at the four kids, "Thank you, volunteers, for helping show us what tidal creatures do to survive."

Michael spoke to the group next. "The pool of water right here is only a semi–tide pool. It has been mixed in with rainwater. But let's start exploring it first. Go sit nearby it and watch for signs of life. Be patient and wait. It may take a moment or two, but I guarantee you will see something."

All the kids walked up to the pool, while the parents either watched or joined their children. James immediately saw a small snail creeping along an underwater rock. "Look," he whispered, "a periwinkle! We've seen these at California beaches, too. This one is really tiny."

Morgan noticed tons of barnacles locked onto the rocks.

Nancy walked over to Morgan. "I want to show you something. The barnacles don't appear alive, but look closely." Nancy waved her hand back and forth in the water, creating small ripples. "When you do that," she explained, "the barnacles react as if the tide is coming in, and they want to eat."

Morgan noticed a group of tiny, feathery legs protruding from the barnacle. "There they are!" Nancy exclaimed. "That's how they gather particles of food from the water."

Morgan then waved her hand back and forth over some other barnacles. Their feathery tops came out of their shells and lapped back and forth in the small current. "Cool!" Morgan said.

A moment later, the rangers gathered everyone together again. "That was just the warm-up!" Michael said. He held up some plastic containers. "Now we really get to find some creatures. But here are some rules for your safety as well as for our tide pool friends. You can't gather a creature that is stuck to rock. That may kill it. Also, please remember where you found each animal because at the end of our time together, we're going to return them to their homes. Another thing, you will need to put ocean water in your container and change it out a few times so it doesn't get too warm. Finally, and this one's important," Michael emphasized, "don't turn your back to the ocean. Parents, please accompany your children for safety, and nobody go beyond where Nancy and I go."

"OK, one last thing," Michael added. "In a little while we're going to meet back here to see what each of us has found."

All the kids took a container and began their search. Morgan and James immediately found a small pool of water, with James instantly reporting, "There are tons of mussels in here!"

Morgan saw several round shells with ridges leading to a volcano-shaped cone. "What are these?" she asked.

Michael came over. "These, my friend, are limpets. They are actually mollusks or sea snails with a conical shape. They're one of my favorite tide pool creatures."

Morgan and James searched on, clambering over barnacle-laden rocks and avoiding the piles of wet, slippery seaweed.

Nancy saw some greenish, stringy seaweed near where the Parkers were searching. "We call that stuff 'mermaid's hair,'" she informed them.

"Neat," Morgan replied, taking a picture of the seaweed.

"Sea urchins over here!" James called out. Morgan, Mom, and Dad carefully scrambled over. The pool had several purple spiny urchins in it.

"Nice find!" Dad commented.

James took one out for his container, placed it in, and then scooped up some water.

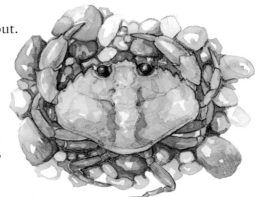

"We got a crab!" a boy called out.

The Parkers looked over. The boy was holding his small tide pool creature in a plastic container, walking toward his mom and dad to show them. As he passed near the Parkers, James asked, "Can I see it?"

The boy diverted to James and Morgan. He proudly lifted his crab, which was scooting along in the plastic container, and announced, "This thing probably hates me right about now."

After Morgan and James examined the crab, the boy went up to his parents.

Morgan found a tiny, slowly moving sea snail, another periwinkle. She plucked it out of the water and into the container. "Don't worry," she spoke to the miniature animal. "I won't keep you in here long."

Meanwhile, Dad tried a new method for searching. He found some small stones right next to a tide pool and carefully rolled one over. "Ah ha!" he called out.

Mom laughed. "I wonder who the kids are around here!"

Meanwhile, Morgan and Mom climbed down to the large lower pool of water. The two rangers and many of the other families were already congregating there. One girl pointed out to her mom, "There's a starfish right behind that floating seaweed over there."

That got the Parkers' attention. They started searching just for sea stars.

Soon, Morgan saw one. It had five thin arms and was an off-white color. Her heart raced with excitement. She reached in and captured the unusual, fragile-appearing sea star. Morgan placed it in her container and added some fresh water. Then she stood up and marched over to Mom.

"Look what I have!"

"Whoa!" Mom replied. "Now that's a cool find."

Just then Michael called out, "OK, everyone. Let's bring what you've got over to the Amphitheater!"

All the families sauntered over to the group's original meeting spot. Each of the children carried their catches carefully. At one point Mom helped Morgan and James across a large crevasse in the rocks. "I don't want you, or your tide pool friends, falling here," she explained.

One by one each of the kids showed what they had found. There were several crabs, lots of sea urchins, periwinkles, and many sea stars shared with the group. But when it got to Morgan's turn, Michael and Nancy each looked amazed. "That," Nancy exclaimed, "is a blood star. They're much less common than regular sea stars."

Nancy picked up the star and showed it to the group. "But this blood star that Morgan found is rare for two reasons. One is that it is very large. Usually they're no larger than a half-dollar, and this one is clearly bigger than that. And the other reason," Nancy glanced at the sea star and smiled at Morgan, "is its color. Blood stars are typically bright orange to red in color. This one, though, is like an albino white. This is way cool, Morgan."

All the kids and many of their parents spent the last few minutes of their time together walking around and examining the collection of creatures.

Finally Michael said, "It's time to say good-bye to our tide pool friends. Please put them back in the exact location as they were found. Then return the plastic container to Nancy or me and say good-bye. It's been great having you attend our Tidepool School!"

The group clapped, then walked off to return their finds.

When Morgan placed her sea star in the water, she said, "Thank you, blood star. Here you are, snugly back at home. I wish you a long and healthy, happy life!"

Morgan stood up and dried her hands on her pants, then clambered up to join her family.

Indiana Jones and Tom Sawyer's Island

The Parkers' quest for hiking adventures in Acadia continued. So they drove to near Jordan Pond and parked for the Bubble Rock Trail hike.

The one-mile trail was an uphill, well-traveled path. The family hiked through the thick birch forest, anticipating the views that lay ahead.

The forest soon gave way to a more-open area on a granite dome called the South Bubble. There Morgan, James, Mom, and Dad stared down at Jordan Pond far below.

Mom gazed at the picturesque body of water. "That's an awfully big pond," she said. "In California we'd call it a lake."

They continued on to Bubble Rock, the famous hanging erratic. Once they arrived, the Parkers examined the precariously perched, giant boulder.

"I wonder how much longer it will stay up there," Morgan mused. "It looks like you could just push it over."

"Gravity will certainly get it at some point," Mom added. "But I wouldn't want to be around here when it happens."

Across the way from Bubble Rock were the cliffs above Jordan Pond. And as it goes in Acadia, there was a trail up there, too. While overlooking Jordan Pond and snacking, James pointed to their next destination. "There's what's waiting!"

Jordan Pond

After hiking back, the family drove to nearby Jordan Pond. Once they found a parking spot in one of Acadia's busiest areas, they waltzed past the teahouse, called Jordan Pond House. James licked his lips. "I can't wait to come back here for treats!" he announced.

The family left the hubbub behind and soon were on the Jordan Cliffs Trail.

"Uh-oh!" Morgan called out a short distance later. She noticed a familiar sign along the trail. Morgan summarized it for her family: "Steep, exposed, and iron rungs."

Mom remained confident. "We'll just see how it goes along the way."

While climbing through a rocky, rooty section of trail, the Parkers were serenaded by the constant chirping of birdsong.

Dad tried to imitate some of the calls by whistling. After several attempts, he glanced at his family. "Not very good, am I?"

"I didn't say anything!" James replied, smirking.

Soon the family's climb led them to a series of cliff-side traverses across narrow granite ledges. "Stay close to the wall!" Mom said repeatedly.

"And watch every step," Dad added to their hiking mantra of the moment.

At one point Dad stopped until everyone had gathered together. "Let's take a little break here and enjoy the views."

The family stood and gazed out at Jordan Pond far below. "It's like an inland fjord down there, a glacially sculpted valley filled in by water," Dad said, admiring the scenery.

Soon the Parkers were back hiking. They kept scrambling, climbing, and traversing. Then they arrived at a long, thin, downward-angled plank of wood with railings to hold onto.

Dad stopped his family at the top of it. "It looks like we're all going to have to walk the plank," he said in his best pirate voice.

Then Dad got serious. "Really, we're going to need to go one at a time in here and slowly."

The family made it down, with Morgan and James having delighted looks on their faces all the way. Morgan said at the bottom, "Hiking in Acadia feels like being in an Indiana Jones movie."

"Or Tom Sawyer's Island at Disneyland," Mom added.

More catwalks and traverses awaited the family. "Hello, iron rungs!" James said at one point to the familiar trail obstacle.

Eventually they passed through the major hurdles along the trail and began following blue-painted streaks on the rocks and cairns to the summit.

Mom commented as they passed a particularly fanciful cairn, "These things each have a little style to them. They're like art on the trail."

Dad added, "Acadia may have some of the best-constructed hiking trails of all the national parks we've been to."

Soon the Parkers arrived at the top of Penobscot Mountain. They celebrated by gathering together for pictures and having a light lunch.

The family spent a few minutes soaking in the views. Cadillac Mountain was in one direction and nearby Sargent Mountain another. Far below was the Jordan Pond House.

The Parkers made a loop trail out of their hike by taking the sloping trail down Penobscot. Later, when they arrived at the Jordan Pond House, they each got a Bar Harbor Bar from the gift shop and sat outside.

"Pretty good!" James grinned after biting into a quickly melting bar and licking the ice cream off his lips.

Ridiculous, but Incredible!

The next day, Morgan, James, Mom, and Dad stepped off the Island Explorer Bus at the Precipice Trailhead. The Parkers approached the ominous warning sign at the base of the hike.

"If you are afraid of heights, think twice before hiking this trail," Morgan announced.

"You climb 930 feet in less than a mile," James added.

Dad also read over and summarized, "This is a nontechnical climbing route, not a hiking trail."

Mom looked at everyone. "I know we've been talking constantly about this trail. And the hikes so far have been fantastic, fun, challenging, and adventurous. But, if any of us doesn't want to go, we can turn around right now and no one will think the worse for it. It is a lot easier to turn back here than anywhere up there. What say you all?"

The Parkers all agreed to go on. "But with one condition," Dad said. "Mom and I will make certain we all go slowly and safely at each step."

Soon they all hoisted themselves up the first of what would be many metal rungs placed along the trail. "That," Dad said, "wasn't easy!"

Immediately after, the family began climbing up a steep gully filled with giant boulders. Familiar blue marks painted on the rocks indicated the best path up. "Just take your time in here," Mom reminded everyone.

The haul up the boulders continued. At one point Mom paused to let everyone rest and gather together. "I think," Mom said, then caught her breath, "this is our decision point. We either turn around here or make it all the way to the top."

"To the top!" James exclaimed, and everyone else agreed.

Soon the Parkers passed a family coming down. "How was it?" Dad inquired.

"Whatever you do, don't come down this trail," the mom answered. "There are several trails around the Precipice at the top. We made a bad decision coming this way."

Dad turned to his family. "Did you get that, everyone?"

The long haul up the incredibly steep boulder field took the Parkers to more metal rungs and railings. "Ah, our old friends," Dad joked.

● ● ●

The Parkers' ascent now was over a series of highly exposed sections. Morgan remarked, "I can sure see where this trail got its name."

Dad decided to coach from the back. "Use three points of contact, everyone. Make sure you've got the grip you need before going on." He stood directly behind Morgan and James, spotting them if needed. But once again, the Parkers passed through the latest obstacle.

At each new challenge, Morgan, James, Mom, and Dad used what they learned from their recent rock climbing in the Tetons.

"I just mantled over that boulder," James said.

"I'm using an under-cling to get up this rock," Mom called out.

Dad announced, "I'm going to chimney up that crevasse."

Finally Morgan said from near the top of another steep pitch, "I'm stemming over here."

But when Morgan hoisted herself over the latest section of vertical ascents, she looked up and said, "Oh, there are plenty more of these above."

"You can't say we weren't properly warned at the start," Mom said, wiping sweat off her forehead.

Dad again spotted for Morgan and James on another ladder with handholds. He said, "This trail kind of reminds me of Angels Landing in Zion and Half Dome in Yosemite. I can't say which of the three is the most difficult, but the Precipice sure is a supreme challenge."

The Parkers kept on. They reached a section Mom named the "Ridiculous Traverse." "There's a huge drop-off at this ledge," she described while staying as far away from it as she could. Mom looked in the direction of the cliff. "I don't want to even think about it."

But she carefully guided Morgan and James across.

Dad, at the back, said, "My hands are sweating and my life depends on my grip. I wish we had some climbing chalk."

The climb continued, with small sections of flatter rock for breaks in between. The Parkers made it to another such place when they came upon a Ridge Runner sitting next to a man. The uniformed trail patrol person said to the man, "Just take some deep breaths. It's OK. We'll just sit right here for a while."

When Morgan, James, Mom, and Dad were all on the same ledge as the man, they took advantage of the brief respite on the rocks. But they also didn't want to crowd the situation.

The man was now shaking while saying repeatedly, "I just don't want to be up here anymore."

Mom whispered to the Ridge Runner, "Is there anything we can do?"

The Ridge Runner shook his head. "No. I've got food and water and a radio," he replied. "We're going to just hang out for a few minutes and go from there."

The last thing the Parkers heard the man say when they climbed on was, "I should have paid more attention to those signs at the start."

"More ledges, climbs, and traverses," Dad called out from the back. Then he added, "This is the hardest, longest nine-tenths of a mile that I've ever done."

Another cliff-hanger traverse greeted the Parkers. "This one is even crazier!" Mom said while cautiously making sure her family crossed it.

"If you need my hand, kids, I'm right here." Mom held out her arm, but the twins made it through without help.

Once the Parkers passed the obstacle, they reached an area where the trail clearly wasn't as steep. Mom looked up and cried out, "I see the summit ahead!"

Soon they were back on a more secure trail, and they passed a sign warning hikers not to go down the Precipice. "We already know about that," James said.

The family followed the blue lines to the summit of 1,058-foot Champlain Mountain. There Morgan gathered her weary but exhilarated family together and said, "Smile, everyone!" Then she snapped several photos.

From Champlain Mountain, the Parkers took the long, slow downhill trail toward the Bowl again. Along the way James called out, "You can see Cadillac Mountain over there!"

Somewhere on the descent, Morgan noticed tiny fruit growing among the low-lying shrubs. "Blueberries!" she exclaimed.

The Parkers indulged, hiked on, and ate some more. Dad mentioned casually while

nibbling on a tiny sweet blueberry, "The Precipice, that was nothing," he laughed. "Bring it on!" Then he looked at his surprised family. "I was just kidding!"

Mom said seriously, "It was a once-in-a-lifetime trail, that's for sure. Morgan and James, you both were amazing on it. "

Eventually the Parkers made it to the Bowl and then Gorham Mountain and finally down to the Ocean Path. There they took the mostly flat trail to Thunder Hole.

Unfortunately, the famous shoreline chasm was just gurgling and sloshing with each gentle, lapping wave.

"Oh well," Morgan said. "You can't always get what you want."

After the hike and the brief time at Thunder Hole, the Parkers caught the next bus back to their campsite at Blackwoods.

Calm water in Thunder Hole

We Made a Beach!

In the bright early-morning light, the Parkers hurried down the stairs at Sand Beach. They were a little late for the Super Sand Sleuths program. Morgan and James joined the group on the beach, while Mom and Dad stood behind and watched.

Ranger Lisa said to the twelve or so students, "The sand here is surprisingly complex. I want all of you to take a scoop of it and put it into these little magnifying containers. Examine the sand, noticing color, texture, and whatever other details you can find."

Morgan and James each took a magnifier. James scooped up some sand and began studying it. "There are green and red flakes," he announced.

"And yellow, white, and brown," Morgan added.

A moment later Lisa said to the group, "The colors come mostly from the crushed shells of sea creatures. That's what's really making the sand. And the waves are doing all the work."

Lisa next had everyone stand in a straight line on the sand. "We're going to be waves," she informed them, "and crush the shells just like waves do. First, everybody, let's jump up and down at least ten times."

All the kids jumped a bunch of times on the sand. Lisa stopped them and said, "You were just crushing the sand, exactly like waves do. If you did that all day long and for years, you might have a similar impact as the waves—they never stop. Imagine how fine the sand would become!"

Lisa went on. "Let's imagine I'm Old Soaker Island out there." The ranger pointed to the small rocky island visible from the beach. "Waves hit it all the time. So we'll pretend you are the waves." Lisa moved a distance away from the group. "And over here near me is the island. When I say 'wave,' run toward me. When I say 'rocks,' stop—you'll be crashing into the rocks around the island."

"OK, wave!"

All the kids ran quickly ahead.

"Rocks!"

Everyone stopped, pretending they were waves smashing into Old Soaker Island.

Lisa gathered everyone around. "Waves not only hit the island, helping to erode the rocks, but they bring something with them. And I am going to show you what it is."

The ranger held up a black rectangular-shaped piece of cloth netting. "Follow me," she said to the group.

Lisa walked toward the small waves crashing on the shore. "I need a few volunteers to help me out. But don't worry, you will all get a chance."

A group of three children came up. Each held a corner of the cloth with Lisa, and they marched toward the water and dipped the cloth down so that a small wave crashed onto it. "Now, lift!" Lisa directed.

They lifted the netting; there was a bunch of sand in it.

After all the kids took a turn, Lisa explained, "When waves batter shells into rocks and rocky shorelines like we have here in Maine, they break down the shells into sand. We call that 'erosion.' The suspended sand is now in the water and eventually gets dumped onto beaches like this. We call that process 'deposition.'"

"Here, let me show you some more." Lisa took a large, clear plastic jug already nearly full with seawater. She very gently scooped in several cups of sand, showing the group two distinct layers, sand at the bottom and water on top.

"Now the waves are coming!" Lisa exclaimed. She shook the jug several times, and everyone saw the cloudy, sandy water inside.

"Yep. That's what you are swimming in here at Sand Beach, sandy water!" Lisa informed the group. "That's one of the reasons we have showers up at the parking lot. But that's if you choose to swim at all. The water temperature right now is about fifty-seven degrees."

"OK," Lisa said. "We have one last thing to do."

The ranger led everyone to the back of the beach, where she had shovels waiting. "Let's find out what's under the sand here. Take a shovel, everyone. Find a safe spot away from others and start digging."

All the kids did so. But they didn't dig for long. Within a few moments several started calling out, "There are rocks down there!"

Morgan and James quickly hit bottom, too.

Lisa gathered the shovels and gave one last bit of information. "Sand Beach wasn't completely like this until recently. In fact, it was an April, Patriot's Day storm in 2007 that deposited a great deal of this sand that we are standing on. Until then, it was quite a bit rockier."

The ranger added, "Given that information, who knows what this beach will look like the next time you are here! We might even have to relocate this program," she laughed.

Lisa looked at the group and said, "Thank you all for coming to Super Sand Sleuths. You were a great class!"

Everyone clapped and said good-bye to the ranger.

After the program, Morgan, James, Mom, and Dad waded in the water at the fluctuating shore. "It's cold!" Dad exclaimed.

The Parkers spent a few more minutes at Sand Beach. Then they walked the Ocean Path up toward Thunder Hole. Instead of going directly to their car, Morgan and James persuaded their parents to return to Thunder Hole. "Maybe the waves are bigger now," James said.

"Look at the crowds," Morgan added. "Something must be going on."

Thunder Hole boomed below, and the Parkers knew this time they were there at the right time. They scurried down the stairs and found a spot along the rails where they, too, could watch the chasm.

In a moment the water in the ocean gully quickly sucked out to sea, draining the chasm to a much lower level. Collectively all the onlookers took a deep breath and watched a large swell funnel into the tight passage. It crashed into the chasm and boomed against the rocks inside the hole. Then a showering curtain of cascading ocean water pummeled and sloshed about the rocks before draining off.

"Whoo-hoo!" James called out. "Way to go, Thunder Hole!"

The Parkers watched four more large waves careen into Thunder Hole before Mom said, "We better go if we want to catch what's next."

They scrambled to their car and drove to the west side of the park at Echo Lake. There they caught the last minutes of the Peregrine Watch on the beach. A ranger pointed out the nesting pair of peregrines on the cliffs above Echo Lake.

PEREGRINES ARE BACK!

For centuries peregrine falcons hunted across all of North America. Using their sharp talons, these predators dove at prey at speeds of over one hundred miles per hour!

By the mid-1960s, however, no breeding peregrines existed anywhere in the eastern United States. Initially nest robbing, trapping, and hunting devastated the peregrine population. But the falcons also ingested pollutants and pesticides, especially from eating toxic songbirds, a primary source of prey. The buildup of toxins in peregrines caused them to not be able to have babies. All of this led to peregrines becoming an endangered species.

The 1973 Endangered Species Act provided for protection of all animals and their habitats that are included on the list. A plan was developed to have a self-sustaining population of peregrines back in the Acadia area. From 1984 to 1986, twenty-two peregrine chicks were hatched in Acadia on the cliffs overlooking Jordan Pond. The first adult nested again in the park in 1991. Now there are several nesting pairs living on Mount Desert Island. The program has been so successful, peregrines have been removed from the endangered species list.

After the group dispersed, the Parkers stayed a few minutes longer, watching the birds in their nest. Mom said to her family, "It's great to see peregrines anywhere!"

The Parkers then swam and rested at the much warmer Echo Lake for the remainder of the day. At one point Dad took a break to hike the nearby Acadia Mountain Trail.

When Dad came back, he was clearly sweating. "How was your hike?" James asked.

"Remote and wonderful," Dad replied. Then he jumped into the lake and swam out to the buoy while James and Morgan followed.

Echo Lake

Rockefeller's Gift

The Parkers took their rented bikes from a shop in downtown Bar Harbor and walked over to the nearby Island Explorer bus stop. There they loaded their bikes on a carrier and got on the bus for Eagle Lake and the carriage roads.

A short time later they got off the bus, unloaded their bikes, and gathered together. Morgan noticed all the other riders also starting their journey on the park's special roads. "It sure is a popular thing to do here," she mentioned.

Out of habit, Dad checked the air pressure in the tires on each of their bikes, then he looked at the twins. "Are we all good to go?"

Morgan and James nodded, and Mom agreed. They put on their helmets and within seconds the family was peddling along the east side of Eagle Lake.

The well-maintained gravel road skirted along the shore of the lake, but also wandered into the forest. The Parkers kept a casual pace, basking in their new park activity and admiring the scenery.

Soon they came to a junction. James checked the map, then said, "It's this way up to Jordan Pond."

The family turned onto the "Around the Mountain" carriage road. As they climbed up a gradual hill, Dad said, "I could do this every day on roads like this."

"And we don't have to worry about cars," James added.

Up ahead, a family had gotten off their bikes and were bent down near the bushes at the side of the road. As Morgan, James, Mom, and Dad approached, they noticed the family picking berries off the small shrubs.

Mom stepped off her bike. "What have you found there?" she said to a young child.

The little girl replied by holding up a tiny berry. "Blueberries!" she exclaimed.

Mom's eyes lit up. "I was hoping we'd find some along here."

Mom put the kickstand down on her bike and called the rest of her family over. "C'mon, it's snack time!"

The Parkers started searching for their own blueberry-filled section of shrubs. "Over here!" Mom called.

Morgan, James, and Dad joined Mom. They started picking, and immediately plunked the ripe blueberries into their mouths. "Mmmm, sweet," James reported.

"The one I just had was a little sour," Morgan admitted.

While the Parkers searched and picked, the little girl from the other family wandered over. "Look at my bag," she said, holding up a plastic baggie with dozens of the delicacies inside.

"Whoa!" Morgan replied. "Lucky you!"

The little girl smiled. "Do you want some?"

"Oh, thank you so much," Morgan beamed. "But just one, since we're picking our own. I don't want to take any from your yummy supply, OK?"

The other family came over and introduced themselves as Mike, Kimberly, and three-year-old Maggie from Boston.

After the Parkers introduced themselves and told where they were from, the mother responded by saying, "Boy, you've come a long way!"

"But it has been so worth it," Dad replied.

James then said, "I'm not able to save the blueberries like you did, Maggie. I just eat them right on the spot."

After each of them had eaten quite a few more, Mom said, "We had best head out now."

They said good-bye to the family just as Maggie was being loaded back into the child carrier behind a bike.

The Parkers pedaled on, eventually getting glimpses of Jordan Pond. "We know what lies ahead!" James exclaimed.

Mom, Dad, James, and Morgan kept a steady pace around the lake. Soon they arrived at the main Jordan Pond area. There they filled up their water bottles, locked their bikes, and got in line for lunch at the Jordan Pond House.

"Popovers await!" Morgan exclaimed.

The Parkers opted for the outdoor tables with views of Jordan Pond and the glacially sculpted North and South Bubbles in the distance.

After indulging in the popovers and a light lunch, the Parkers returned to their bikes and rode on. Their trail took them to the majestic Jordan Pond Gate House. They stared at the stately building. "Looking at that makes me feel like we've stepped back in time," Dad said.

Morgan snapped several photos. They passed by the gate and were back on the carriage roads again.

The road meandered into the forest, climbing steadily but not steeply. After a good several miles of riding, the Parkers came to another body of water, Bubble Pond. The serene pond was nestled in a bowl surrounded by Acadia's forested domes of rock.

Mom said while pedaling, "This just might be my favorite spot of our whole ride today!"

Acadia's carriage roads were designed to draw attention to nature and the natural surroundings. The roads were located so that they would blend with the landscape around them. Trees were saved when possible, and island granite was used in the construction. John D. Rockefeller Jr. directed and paid for the building of the roads so that people who visited Acadia would be able to enjoy the park's lakeshores, forests, wetlands, and valleys. They were designed to meander from place to place without having specific destinations to lead people to. Rockefeller also built seventeen stone-crafted bridges among the carriage roads as well as gatehouses like the one at Jordan Pond.

James added, remembering where Bubble Pond was on the map, "You know, if we didn't ride our bikes out here, we may never have come to this pond."

The Parkers rode to the north end of the large pond. There they got off their bikes and walked up to the gravely shoreline. Morgan noticed signs prohibiting swimming. "There's always Echo Lake!" she said.

Meanwhile, Morgan was also noticing something in the water near shore. "Look—giant pollywogs!"

The family came over and saw several especially large pollywogs in the shallow waters. "That one is already growing legs," James said. "It'll soon become a frog."

After hanging out at the pond for some time, the family pedaled on, soon returning to the much larger Eagle Lake, but this time on the eastern shore.

They rode along Eagle Lake and eventually returned to the parking lot where the bus originally dropped them off. After they got off their bikes, Mom said, "This has been my favorite of all our days here in Acadia."

James took out his map and showed Mom. "It doesn't have to end yet." He pointed out on the map the short carriage road loop circling Witch Hole Pond to the north.

"Let's do it!" Dad exclaimed.

The Parkers got back on their bikes, rode underneath the highway, and pedaled on.

Eagle Lake

While passing the small body of water called Breakneck Ponds, Dad said, "I think this is the most scenic and pleasant fifteen or so miles I have ever ridden."

Just then Morgan called out, "I found the mother lode of blueberries!" She quickly ditched her bike and dashed over to the shrubs.

The family spent quite some time picking and eating again. After a while, James said, "How many of these are we allowed to take in a day, anyway?"

"Up to a gallon per person," Dad replied.

"OK, then we can still eat some more," Morgan said.

When they got back on their bikes, Mom said, "You just have to be grateful to Rockefeller for setting up these roads. They're such a unique and great gift to the park and to all of us."

As the family rode around Witch Hole Pond, they noticed a few beaver lodges in the distance. Then they saw a small group of people with nets sloshing in a marsh, trying to catch things.

The Parkers rode up and watched a ranger pluck a frog from the pond. He took several pictures of the amphibian and wrote something down in a log book. He released the creature where he found it before resuming the search for other living things.

Mom was curious. "Can I ask what you are doing out here?"

The ranger answered, "We're on a twenty-four-hour BioBlitz. We're identifying species of life in selected areas and documenting what we find."

"What have you found so far?" James asked.

"Well, last year in our BioBlitz, we noted over three hundred types of moths in the park, including several species that were unknown to scientists until we discovered them here. This year, though, we're focusing on aquatic insects. But we just got started in this area, so who knows what we'll find."

The ranger picked up on the Parkers' keen interest. "You know, anyone can volunteer to help do this. If you are interested, just get information from the park visitor center or our website for future BioBlitzes."

"Oh, we absolutely will," Mom replied.

The Parkers watched the BioBlitz for a few more minutes. Then they continued their loop around Witch Hole Pond and eventually back to Eagle Lake. After waiting a few minutes, the bus came. They loaded their bikes and climbed inside.

Once seated, Dad said, "Well, that was quite a day!"

The Adventures of Mini-Ed

After a quiet morning in camp, the Parkers made their way back through Bar Harbor and onto the campus of the College of the Atlantic. There they found the pier leading them to the boat *Starfish Enterprise*. They boarded with about twenty-five other passengers for the Dive-In Theater.

"Hey," Morgan said while her family found seats. "There's the family we saw yesterday picking blueberries on the carriage road."

As soon as everyone was seated, a man introduced himself as "Diver Ed." He then introduced his crew, which included his wife, known on board as "Captain Evil," a national park ranger, several other crew members, and two large black Newfoundland dogs he called Newfies.

Then Diver Ed gave a life jacket demonstration, using one of the large dogs.

As the boat headed out to sea, the ranger narrated their unique tour. She pointed out birds, islands, a porpoise gliding along the ocean surface, lobster buoys, views of Mount Desert Island, and other features of the Gulf of Maine.

Somewhere out at sea, near small, rockbound Egg Rock Island, Diver Ed began to don his wet suit and gear.

"He's getting ready," Dad said with anticipation.

Captain Evil began slowing the boat down.

But before the much-anticipated events developed further, Captain Evil turned the boat so the passengers could see the lighthouse on the island. The ranger pointed out two bald eagles on the rocks near shore. She also pointed to a dozen or so harbor seals in the water nearby.

"They're poking their heads out of the water and looking right at us!" Morgan observed.

Soon the boat completely stopped, and the crew lowered an anchor.

Diver Ed stepped in front of the passengers, and while putting on the rest of his gear, he explained, "I need this weight belt to help me go lower in the water. Without it, I would be too buoyant to get to the bottom."

Diver Ed also pointed out the valve that would regulate the pressure as he dove down and returned to the surface.

Next Diver Ed said a microphone and a camera would accompany him on his journey. "With all this equipment," he said while looking at a large television screen mounted on the boat above his head, "you'll be able to see every creature I encounter and all the dangers I face under the sea." Diver Ed lifted up a camera with lights attached to it, so the audience could see how they would view his underwater adventure.

Then Diver Ed donned his mask and smiled through all the gear.

"Hey, Everyone! Make a clear path for Diver Ed!" Captain Evil called out.

Diver Ed

Diver Ed waltzed to the back of the boat, turned to the audience, waved, and fell backwards into the ocean.

Captain Evil told everyone that Diver Ed was connected to a six-hundred-foot cable, so that he was never really detached from the boat.

Once Diver Ed was underwater, the passengers focused their attention on the TV screen. A moment later, Diver Ed showed himself on camera, waved, and said cheerfully, "Hello, everyone!"

Captain Evil now narrated the journey. "Diver Ed's heading to the ocean bottom," she said while referring to the screen. "You can see that everything is becoming green and dark."

Mini-Ed

Diver Ed turned on a light, then he introduced everyone to someone else. "Say hi to my friend, 'Mini-Ed.'" He held up a small plastic scuba figure to the camera.

All the passengers waved hello to Mini-Ed.

Captain Evil explained. "Diver Ed gets lonely down there," she joked. "But, really, he uses Mini-Ed to show perspective. We can see how big the creatures at the bottom of the ocean are by comparing them to Mini-Ed, who is just three inches long, or about the size of an adult finger."

Diver Ed called out, "I'm at the bottom now. It's forty-two feet deep, and I've already got a cool blood star!"

Diver Ed dropped Mini-Ed by the blood star. Mini-Ed landed right next to the whitish deep-sea echinoderm. They were about the same size.

Captain Evil commented, "Nice find, Diver Ed!"

Diver Ed picked up the blood star and turned it over. In his other hand he took Mini-Ed and had it "kiss" the blood star on its "mouth," as Diver Ed said. Then he plunked the ocean creature into a netted bag.

James leaned over to Morgan. "That blood star looked just like the one you found."

Morgan smiled. "I know. For a moment I thought it might be the same one!"

Diver Ed spoke into the microphone. "Look at these cool shrimp down here." He held the camera to show a group of orangish yellow shrimp moving on a rock.

"Way to go, Diver Ed!" Captain Evil said to her husband. Then she told the passengers, "They're actually skeleton shrimp, pretty amazing. They're scuttling along that rock like a bunch of underwater praying mantises."

Diver Ed spoke again. "I've got a lobster down here!" He turned the camera to a dark and jagged crevasse between the rocks.

Captain Evil told the audience, "Lobsters love to hide among the rocks, especially when they shed their shells. We like to call those underwater cracks and rocks 'lobster condominiums.'"

Captain Evil asked, "Are you going to try and get the lobster?"

"Not yet," Diver Ed replied. "Look at what's on the rock!"

Diver Ed pointed the camera to an orange sea star with one long arm and four clearly shorter ones. He took it off the rock, then placed the sea star into the net.

Captain Evil told the crowd, "That sea star has lost at least four arms in its life. Those shorter arms are all being regenerated."

Diver Ed said, "Now I'm going after that lobster—it's huge!"

He pointed the camera at the crustacean just peeking out of its nook. The passengers could see the top of one of its claws, its tiny beady eyes, and the orange, green, and yellow colors of its shell.

Captain Evil said, "It's a big lobster, Diver Ed. Are you sure you want to do this?"

Diver Ed replied, "Let me send Mini-Ed down there first to scope out the situation."

The passengers on the boat cruise watched Mini-Ed drop down, right in front of the lobster's den, and land on the ocean bottom.

The lobster flinched backward, then crept forward right toward the plastic figure. Suddenly it reached out an enormous claw and clamped onto Mini-Ed, instantly tearing off a piece of the toy figure.

Diver Ed screamed, "Mini-Ed has been attacked! I'm going to have to put the camera down."

Diver Ed dropped the camera onto the ocean floor. Between that, Diver Ed's quick movements, and the lobster's assault on the plastic figure, all the audience could see was a cloud of sand mixing with the water.

Amid the turmoil, Diver Ed spoke. "Don't worry, Mini, I'm going to rescue you!"

Then after more tumult, Diver Ed said, "I found his mask and head."

"Is he OK?" Captain Evil asked with concern.

For a moment all was quiet. Then Diver Ed reported, "I think I can fix him. Hold on."

The passengers continued to watch the screen showing the dark, green ocean bottom. Then a jerky movement indicated that Diver Ed was picking up the camera. He held up Mini-Ed in front of the camera and said, "He's made an amazing, quick, and full recovery!"

The passengers on the boat cheered and clapped.

Mom turned to Dad. "This is so fun! I'm glad we came." Then she looked at the twins. "I think they're glad, too."

Diver Ed said, "This lobster, though, is huge! I'm going to try to catch it to show all of you on board. But I need both of my hands. I'm going to have to put the camera down again."

Again the audience waited while the screen showed a school of fish swimming in the distance. Captain Evil said, "Those are pollock. It's pretty rare to see so many all in one spot."

Just then Diver Ed called out, "I've got it!"

He picked up the camera and showed the monstrous-size lobster. It was waving its claws right in front of Diver Ed, trying to grab his mask.

Diver Ed worked quickly to get the lobster into the net.

"Way to go, Diver Ed!" Captain Evil exclaimed.

Next Diver Ed pointed the camera to an old, dented, abandoned lobster trap at the bottom of the ocean. "There's a lobster in it!" Diver Ed said. "But I'm going to leave him alone."

Captain Evil explained. "That trap clearly isn't in use anymore. But there sure are lots of lobsters in Maine's waters. One of the reasons why is that their predators have mostly been fished out. Their only real enemy now is humans. So lobsters here are abundant."

Diver Ed now reported, "I'm forty-six feet below and the water temperature is fifty-two degrees." He focused the camera on a purple sea urchin and a crab decorated with seaweed all over its shell. He then put both in the bag.

Captain Evil explained, "Those crabs pick up just about anything they can to put on themselves as camouflage."

Diver Ed held up another creature. "This is one mean-looking crab!" he beamed. The crab had only one claw, but it still looked menacing. Diver Ed placed it in the bag.

Next Diver Ed found some live sand dollars, echinoderms, that he added to the collection.

Diver Ed spoke. "I'm going to come up now."

Morgan and James went to the side of the boat to watch for Diver Ed's return. Soon they saw a bunch of bubbles rise to the surface followed by Diver Ed and his gear. "Here he comes!" Morgan reported.

Once Diver Ed clambered back on board, everyone cheered his homecoming. Diver Ed high-fived several of the kids, including James and

Morgan, while he waddled up to the front of the boat. Then he yanked off his mask, smiled, and exclaimed, "Welcome back, everyone!"

The passengers all laughed.

Diver Ed, Captain Evil, and the ranger quickly set up touch tanks for the newfound creatures. Diver Ed personally rubber-banded the lobster to protect people from its monster-size claws. "These could easily snap a finger off," he explained. "Just remember what it did to Mini-Ed down there."

Diver Ed quickly measured the giant crustacean. "Twenty-four inches!" he reported. "And far too big for a lobsterman to keep."

The passengers gathered around the touch tanks. Everyone on board, especially the children, touched, held, pet, and took pictures of the ocean creatures. Morgan and James noticed Maggie holding Mini-Ed. "Look," Morgan whispered.

Mom came over with Morgan's camera and directed, "You and James hold up that lobster!"

A FUTURE WITH LOBSTERS

The state of Maine has very specific laws to make sure there will be lobsters to harvest in the future. It is an extremely important industry to the region. Therefore, there are minimum- and maximum-size lobster catch limits. A lobster's minimum size must be at least three and a quarter inches in its carapace, or main shelled body area. This is to ensure every lobster has at least one chance to breed in its lifetime before being taken. A maximum-size lobster is five inches in its carapace. Larger lobsters are left to live because they are wanted in the gene pool.

The twins held up the banded lobster while Mom snapped several photos. After they put it back in the touch tank, James said, "Those claws were about as big as my head."

A few minutes later, Diver Ed announced, "We're going to have to say good-bye to our ocean creatures now."

Diver Ed held up the giant lobster and unhooked the bands. "OK, everyone," he said, "say good-bye and I love you, ocean creatures!"

The audience echoed, "Good-bye! I love you, ocean creatures."

He let the children take the crabs, sea stars, urchin, and sand dollars and toss them all overboard. Then Diver Ed tossed the lobster overboard and it was instantly out of sight.

The crew pulled up anchor and took the passengers back to port. Along the way, Dad said, "Well, that was one boat ride I'll never forget."

While they were walking off the boat, Morgan and James approached Maggie. Morgan asked her, "Have you found any more blueberries lately?"

Maggie looked up at Morgan. "Yes," she answered, "but I also have this."

She held up a plastic bag with Mini-Ed in it and said, "We bought it from that person on the boat!"

Island Bound

The Parkers reluctantly left Mount Desert Island and the main part of Acadia behind.

"Some people, I hear, like Isle au Haut better than where we have been," Dad said.

"I don't know if that's even possible," Mom replied.

The family drove the windy, hilly roads to the quaint, ocean-side town of Stonington. They quickly found the dock, parked the car nearby, pulled out all their gear, and picked up the mail boat ferry to Isle au Haut. Many others were also on board: some with bikes, some with just what they needed for the day, and others, like the Parkers, with all the food and camping gear necessary for several days on the island.

As the mail boat left the dock, Mom said, "Only five campsites are on this island, and we have one of them for three nights. We are very lucky!"

The boat ride passed other islands and an ocean full of colorful buoys. James pictured Isle au Haut on a United States map. "We are going about as far as we can get from San Luis Obispo while still on US soil," he said.

"What about Alaska or Hawaii?" Morgan asked.

"I don't know," James replied. "I'll have to measure it out later."

As they cruised along, two porpoises popped up nearby, gliding in and out of the water's surface.

"A good omen," Mom said, leaning into Dad.

Far off, James caught a peek of a spray of water coming from the ocean. He called out. "Is that a whale out there?"

James pointed to where he thought he saw spouting, but there was nothing. "I don't know," he said. "I thought I saw water spray up in the air."

The Parkers watched where James told them to, but after a few minutes, they all resumed looking elsewhere.

Just then a large whale thrust itself high above the water in a grand, twisting, glorious breach before plunging back to the ocean with a massive splash.

"Whoa!" Morgan responded. She looked at James then at her parents wide-eyed, while the passengers on board collectively gasped.

Mom said, "That is something I only expect to see on a televised nature program. And we just witnessed it in person!"

Soon the mail boat approached large and forested Isle au Haut. It stopped first at the small village, and some of the passengers got off. The boat pulled out and continued on to Duck Harbor, where the Parkers, along with several others, exited the boat.

The family hauled their gear off the pier and up to the nearby campground, quickly choosing campsite #4.

Mail boat ferry

At their shelter the Parkers were tucked into the forest, but Duck Harbor was just below, visible through breaks in the trees.

Their site had a three-sided wooden shelter with a floor for their tent. "We could sleep right on the wood," Mom said, "but I hear the bugs come

Our campsite

out later, so I think it is best to set up the tent."

There was also a picnic table and fire pit right outside and a food box in the back.

The Parkers unpacked and set up all their supplies, and soon their little dwelling looked cozy and comfortable. "Our home away from home," Mom mentioned.

After a quick lunch, the family walked the path and dirt road to the water pump. It was a good distance away, and the Parkers would make many more trips there to retrieve water over the next few days.

Later that afternoon the family explored the Western Head and Cliff Trails. They stopped often to investigate beaches and coves as well as to check out tide pools, listen to waves, search for shells, and find abandoned buoys. It was a leisurely pace and without any real agenda.

"We're on an island, so we should have an island pace. No hurries and no worries," Mom said.

After dinner a thick fog rolled in, changing the family's sunset plans. The nearby cove and the forests all around became enshrouded in the low-lying cloud cover. "I can hardly see the dock," Dad reported. "But that sailboat is still clanging out there somewhere."

The family decided to sit by their campfire after dinner. Soon the Parkers, lulled by the ocean sounds and the cool evening, went to bed.

•••

Day two on the island broke clear. Dad took advantage of it by hiking rugged Duck Harbor Mountain. Meanwhile, Mom, James, and Morgan explored more coves, beaches, and tide pools along the nearby Eben's Head Trail. They all reported back to camp just before noon.

View from Duck Harbor Mountain

"It was only a three-hundred-or-so-foot elevation gain," Dad described the hike. "But as things go in Acadia, it was rough, rugged, and wonderful. And the views at the top of the mountain were amazing."

"We had some great views, too," James said of Eben's Head. "And we explored a bunch of rocky beaches. We saw crabs and some washed-up buoys, and a seal was on one of the rocks, sunbathing. We stayed far away, though, and gave it lots of space."

In the afternoon the family walked the four-mile dirt road into town. There they picked up a few groceries and took advantage of a lobster bake right in the village.

"We had to try lobster at some point while we were in Maine," Morgan said after dipping some of the white meat into melted butter.

The family walked back to camp with their bag of food in the early evening. This night, the weather remained clear and warm.

"Our summer evenings in San Luis Obispo are so often cool with the fog rushing in. Tonight here, though, it's warm and sultry. It almost feels tropical, which is kind of nice," Mom said.

The family roasted marshmallows and played cards at their table before walking down to the bluff to watch the sunset.

Later, James commented, "What a great day!" Morgan, Mom, and Dad each smiled their agreement.

•••

On their third day away from the mainland, Dad convinced the family that they needed to hike Duck Harbor Mountain. "If I want to hike it twice," he reasoned, "you'll want to be up there at least once."

"I don't need any convincing," Mom said.

"Let's go!" Morgan and James called out in unison.

The family took the long way around to the mountain trail by first going out again along the Cliff Trail. By the time they reached wild and wavy Deep Cove, it was lunchtime and they found a spot on some rocks to pull out their food.

After lunch, they each took off their shoes on the rocky beach and tried to get into the water. But it was difficult timing the waves, and the water was deep and colder than expected, despite the warm day. After several attempts, Dad just plunged in. He came up grinning and with soaked clothes. "Boy, that felt good!" he exclaimed.

Dad requested some time to dry off, so the family hung out and explored Deep Cove's rocky shoreline.

The Parkers made their way over to the Duck Harbor Mountain Trail, coming from the east side.

Eventually Morgan, James, Mom, and Dad made it to the top and admired the 360-degree views Dad had spoken so highly of.

"The trees are a little stunted up here," Mom mentioned. "Winter weather must blast this area."

"It's just so different than the dry summers in California," Morgan said, thinking of the brown grasses that cover the hills this time of year where the Parkers live.

"Speaking of dry," Dad said, "it looks like our good weather could be ending." He gestured to the dark clouds in the skies toward the south. "A storm is brewing. I can see it and feel it in my bones." Then Dad joked, "Must be from all my days at sea."

The Parkers spent a few more minutes at the summit, scanning the horizon, both for the views and for what the atmosphere appeared to be delivering to the island. Then the wind started picking up. Far off at sea, the Parkers could see whitecaps coming from the swelling waves. Meanwhile the skies darkened further, now blocking the sun completely.

As the breezes started shifting to powerful gusts of wind, Mom remembered, "We don't have the rain fly up! Driving rain can definitely get into our shelter."

And with that, the Parkers started hiking, a little faster, back to camp.

Meanwhile, on a lobster boat somewhere between Stonington and Isle au Haut, the captain on board observed the developing whitecaps, large swells, and gusting winds. He said to his crew, "I'm going to check the weather again for an update."

The captain switched on his marine-band weather radio and heard this broadcast:

> Tropical Storm Ophelia, formerly Hurricane Ophelia, is moving north along the Atlantic Seaboard and toward the Gulf of Maine. Although the storm is losing some of its energy as it moves over cooler waters, there is still a lot of punch to this intense tropical system. Due to that, a tropical storm warning has been issued for all craft in the Gulf of Maine. Winds are soon expected to reach twenty-

five to forty-five knots, with higher gusts likely. In addition, large ocean swells of eight to twelve feet will be common, with some swells reaching up to fifteen feet. Periods of very heavy rain will accompany the storm. Expect all this to begin in the next two to four hours. The storm will reach its peak at or around midnight and taper off rapidly after that. Therefore all marine vessels should . . .

The captain turned off the radio. "OK, everyone," he directed. "*Back to shore!*"

The Parkers returned to camp just as the first few large drops of rain began plunking down. Like a crew at sea, they each went to work quickly to secure and keep as dry as possible everything at their campsite shelter. Mom and Dad put up the rain fly while Morgan and James put away all shelved items, pots, pans, and hanging clothes.

It was now 6:00 p.m. and the scattered showers continued, with the wind whipping about. The family fixed a quick and easy meal. As they were finishing, the first of many downpours ensued.

The pouring rain was driven sideways with pummeling blasts of wind. As the family scrambled to clean up their campsite, James said, "Has it ever rained like this in California?"

"Probably once or twice," Dad replied.

All the Parkers could do once they stashed their dishes in the food box was to go into the tent. It was mostly dry inside, but the wind rattled and shook their little home and rain sprayed onto the roof of the shelter.

"It's going to be a long night," Mom said.

"You think it will blow over by tomorrow?" Dad asked.

"I don't even want to think about tomorrow yet," Mom replied. But she was thinking about it anyway. Her friend, Karen, was going to kayak out with another friend, bringing Mom's boat. Then the other friend would take the ferry back with Dad and the twins, while Mom and Karen kayaked back to Stonington. It was all planned out. That is, at least until the storm. Impossible in this weather, that Mom knew.

Just before what would have been sunset, the Parkers took turns dashing to the bathroom. As each returned, they shared the conditions.

"The wind was blowing me sideways."

"I'm soaked from head to toe."

"At least this shelter is helping our cause."

Finally James said, "The cove is rocking with waves!"

"It's a fierce storm," Mom said. "I have to admit, there's no way Karen and I will even try to kayak in these conditions. But I just hope she's OK. Her plans were to paddle out here first thing in the morning." Then Mom reassured herself. "But I know Karen. She leads kayak tours out here. She's extremely conscientious about safety and always pays attention to the weather. She'll be OK tonight. We'll figure out tomorrow, tomorrow."

With that, the Parkers tried to wait out the storm by sleeping. But the wind and rain didn't quit. It was a long night.

• • •

Sometime early in the morning, James was the first to wake up. It was still and quiet outside and getting light. He heard birds chirping in the forest.

James silently crept outside. Indeed, it was a brand-new day. Streaks of sunlight slanted through the forest, and drops of water glistened off the flora. James tiptoed down to the clearing below camp to assess the cove. His feet squished with each step along the way.

It was a brand-new day down there as well. James dashed up to camp to report the good news.

Mom was awake and outside when James returned. "Clear skies. Sunny. Wind calm and the water, glossy and still."

Mom smiled. "Yea! If all goes as planned, Karen will be here about eight o'clock."

Return to the Mainland

Mom stood high up on the pier at Duck Harbor. After waiting a while, she finally spotted two kayaks paddling into the cove. Right away Mom recognized her old friend from college, Karen.

"Hey there!" Mom called out, waving.

Karen waved back as she and her companion paddled the boats farther into the cove. When they got closer, Karen looked up at Mom, still standing on the pier. "Hey, old buddy," she said, grinning. "I'll meet you on the shore over there."

Karen and her friend maneuvered their boats to a sandy spot, while Mom walked off the pier and called out to her family. "They're here!"

Morgan, James, and Dad hustled down from camp and met Mom with her friend at the gravelly beach.

As soon as Karen landed, she pulled the skirt off the main hatch of the kayak. Using her paddle for support, she balanced herself then stepped out. She walked right up to Mom, giving her a big hug.

The two old friends backed up a step, both still smiling. Then they said at the same time, "You haven't changed a bit."

Mom introduced her family.

Karen then said, "This is Ann," and pointed to her friend hauling up the other boat. "She was kind enough to paddle out with me yesterday. She's got your boat and will take the ferry back with the rest of your clan."

"We were worried about you yesterday," Mom said. "How did you get out here with that storm?"

"Oh that," Karen replied nonchalantly. "It was nothing," she added with a laugh. "Seriously, you're right. That was a crazy storm—a remnant hurricane, in fact. I knew it was coming, so we left early and stayed with a friend over in the village of Isle au Haut. It was the only way it could possibly work."

Karen gazed at the clear blue skies this morning. "But the weather sure has cooperated for us today!"

Everyone spent a few minutes chatting. Then Karen began to get Mom ready for the eight-mile ocean jaunt back to Stonington.

"OK, Kristen," Karen started. "We need to get going soon to give us plenty of time to get to the mainland, so let me tell you about the kayak."

Karen pointed out the sealed hatches for stowing gear and keeping out water, the emergency supplies she had on board, techniques for getting into the boat and out onto the water, and some of the initial paddling strokes.

Mom smiled. "You really have it all dialed in. And that's quite a craft for me."

Karen smiled back. "Welcome to my world as a Master Sea Kayak Guide in Maine. I'm known locally as Kayak Karen. So tell me what kind of kayaking experiences and instruction you've had."

"Oh, here and there on some small lakes and out at the spit by Morro Bay," Mom said. "But never in open water like we're doing. This will definitely be a first for me."

Karen responded, "I'm glad to take you out. And it will give us a chance to fill in the details of the last twenty years of our lives." Karen looked at Morgan and James. "I'll get your mom back to Stonington later this afternoon around two or three o'clock. You'll see us paddling in right next to where you'll be landing earlier." She then said to Mom, "Let's get you on board. We can go over some more techniques while we're out at sea."

Karen helped Mom move the kayak so it was mostly in the water. Then she balanced it so Mom could step in. Once Mom was seated, they both pulled the skirt all the way around the hatch until it was fully secure. Then Karen pushed Mom out into the water.

Mom paddled around nearby, waiting for Karen. When they both were offshore, they looked toward the beach.

"Bon voyage!" Morgan called out while taking pictures.

"See you in Stonington!" James added.

And with that, Mom and Karen began paddling out of the cove. James, Morgan, and Dad watched until they turned right and were out of sight. Then they went up to camp to pack up and haul their gear down to the pier to wait for the mail boat.

As Mom and Karen kayaked along, they took some time to get reacquainted. After filling each other in with the details of their lives, Mom said, "I can't believe that much time, and life, has gone by."

Karen watched Mom paddle along for a few minutes. Then she said, "Would you mind if I gave you a few tips to help your paddling?"

"Not at all," Mom replied. "I'm all ears."

"OK," Karen said. "First, let's fine-tune your hand positions. With your paddle on your head, place your hands far enough apart on the shaft so that your elbows form ninety-degree angles." Karen watched Mom get the paddle in its proper place. "Awesome! That will give you a strong, stable position. You also want to hold the paddle out from your body with nice, straight arms. This is called the 'paddler's box.' As you paddle, use your whole body for efficient paddling."

Mom adjusted her hold on the paddle. "How's that?"

"There, much better," Karen said. "As you paddle, you can use your leg strength, too. With every stroke, try pushing on the same side's stationary foot pedal. As you are stroking, straighten and bend your legs like you're riding a bike and see what happens."

Mom started pedaling and paddling. "Wow!" she responded. "That really got me accelerating."

"A little technique can go a long way. Also, your stroke should go into the water near your feet. Your main power is from your feet to your hips. When you paddle like that, we can really get moving."

Karen watched Mom for a moment then added, "Try drawing an arc with your paddle, out from the boat to just under the surface of the water, not straight down. If you want to turn, follow the arc through to the stern, or back, of the kayak."

"Thanks," Mom said, concentrating. "I'm already feeling the difference."

As Mom and Karen cruised along the water side by side, a lobster boat passed by farther out from shore. Karen turned toward Mom. "We're going to get some waves from that boat. Let's turn right into them and paddle through them. That's the best way to handle oncoming waves."

Sure enough, a series of larger swells created by the boat quickly headed toward Mom and Karen. Mom turned her kayak so that she was heading right toward the swells.

"Paddle right into the waves!" Karen reminded her friend.

Mom paddled strongly forward toward each of the swells. The first wave lifted Mom's kayak high up, then it dipped until the second and third swells rolled by. Soon, both Mom and Karen were beyond the wake.

"Whoo-hoo!" Mom called out once she was in calmer waters. "That was fun!"

"And you handled the kayak perfectly," Karen replied.

Mom and Karen paddled along the shoreline past a lighthouse. "Hugging the shore keeps us out of open water where we are more vulnerable," Karen explained.

Mom noticed a large bird glide toward the water ahead of her. The bird swooped down to the surface and plucked up a fish in its talons. The predator turned its prey facing forward and began to fly away.

"That's an osprey!" Mom called out.

Suddenly a loud piercing call grabbed the kayakers' attention. Another bird, a much larger one, flew toward the osprey. It was a bald eagle, and it started dive-bombing the osprey repeatedly.

After several feigned attacks, the osprey released its fish. The eagle immediately dove and caught the stunned fish right before it hit water. Then the larger bird flew away with its food.

Mom looked at Karen. "Boy, you don't get to see that every day!"

"No, you don't," Karen replied. But she was now eyeing two kayakers, paddling one after the other toward the middle of more-open water.

Karen watched the two move along for a minute. Then she turned toward Mom. "Can you head to that island over there?" she asked.

Karen watched as Mom paddled toward a stark, sandy beach.

Karen smiled at Mom, then took off paddling after the two kayakers. After a moment Karen called back to Mom, "Would you mind staying there? That's our lunch spot anyway. And by the way, I have it all taken care of for you."

As Mom's kayak struck bottom, she placed her paddle behind her and balanced herself on it so she could step out. Once out of the boat, she pulled the kayak farther up on the beach. Karen was now chatting with the kayakers out at sea.

A moment later, Karen turned her kayak toward Mom. She heard Karen call out good-bye to the other kayakers, and they began to paddle toward shore now in a parallel formation.

When Karen reached the tiny island where Mom was, she too beached her kayak. Then Karen waltzed up to Mom.

"What was that all about?" Mom asked.

"I just wanted to help them and make sure they don't get in over their heads. They may not be aware of the constant boat traffic in this area. Just sharing a little local knowledge!"

"What were they doing?"

"Paddling into the middle of a boating lane. Going too far from shore. And kayaking one after another, not side by side. Boats can't see them as well that way."

Mom said, "I'm glad I'm with you, learning the rules of the road. I know I couldn't have done this on my own."

"I'm glad you're with me, too," Karen said. "Besides, look at what I have for us."

Karen opened up one of the hatches on her kayak, then reached in and pulled out a dry bag. She took the bag to a rock and spread out a display of food from inside it. "Lunch is served on Burnt Island!" she announced.

The two hungry kayakers dove right in.

Flipped!

After lunch and a quick dip in the ocean, Mom and Karen were back at it. "We are still less than halfway back to Stonington," Karen said to Mom as they got back in their kayaks. "We have a lot of paddling ahead."

Karen led Mom toward a boulder-strewn area near another small, white, sandy beach and island. She warned Mom, "It's rocky in here and quite shallow. Follow my path as we maneuver between the obstacles."

As Karen and Mom paddled through, Mom saw several large boulders just beneath and sticking above the water's surface. She tapped one with her paddle to test the depth as she glided by.

In the distance, a boat whisked by in the deeper waters. Mom noticed a set of large swells develop in the boat's wake and roll toward her.

The largest swell came quickly. Mom positioned her kayak to take the wave straight on. But, just as she was turning forward, she noticed a large rock barely submerged ahead of her. *I'll hit bottom!* Mom feared.

At the last second, Mom shifted her paddling to try to move to the left, hoping to avoid the rock. Just then the first of the set of swells arrived. But Mom was no longer facing forward against the oncoming waves.

The large, quickly moving swell lifted Mom's kayak, jostling it sideways and directly onto a rock partially sticking up out of the water.

She slammed into the rock, tipping her kayak sideways and rolling her into the ocean.

Instantly Mom was pinned underneath the kayak. Panicked, she did her best to recall Karen's self-rescue steps. *Tuck, pound, pull, and push!* Mom immediately told herself.

While upside down and underwater, Mom bent her body over and tucked in toward the kayak. Then she quickly pounded on the boat. A fleeting second later, she moved her hands up until she found the kayak's skirt still in place and holding her underwater. Mom guided her hands to the front of the hatch, found the grab loop, pulled the skirt off, and pushed herself out of the kayak and into the water. Her life jacket brought her right to the surface. Once her head was above the water, she gasped for breath.

As soon as Mom looked around, she saw Karen already in contact with her kayak. "Are you OK?"

Mom nodded, but Karen could tell she was uncertain. Mom was shivering. "Hold onto your kayak, and I'll get you away from these rocks," Karen instructed.

Karen swiftly attached a carabiner to Mom's kayak and guided it away from any rocks. Once they were clear of the underwater obstacles, Karen told Mom to hold onto her kayak while she lifted the bow on Mom's craft over to hers to empty the water from the cockpit. Then Karen placed the kayak back into the water and stabilized it while talking Mom through the steps that would lead her back in.

After getting Mom back into the boat, Karen towed Mom's kayak between several rock obstacles and paddled the two safely toward Wheat Island, only ten or so yards away. In little time, they hit land on the tiny island. Karen noticed that Mom's lips were tinting blue.

After the kayaks were partially onshore, Karen hustled over and helped Mom out. She held her up and walked her to the beach, sitting her down propped up against a rock.

Karen dashed back to the boats and pulled them farther up on the sand. Then she rushed over to Mom, who was shivering even more.

"Quite a spill you had there!" Karen said, trying to speak matter-of-factly.

"You . . . can . . . say . . . that . . . again," Mom said between chattering teeth.

Mom was clearly cold and possibly borderline hypothermic. In addition, she could be hurt and likely frightened—all due to her tumble into the Gulf of Maine.

"First," Karen directed, "we need to get you into some warm, dry clothes. I have an emergency set of clothes in a dry bag in my kayak."

Karen helped Mom get out of her wet gear. Then she wrapped Mom in a dry towel. After that, Mom was able to put on Karen's extra set of dry clothes.

From that point Mom improved rapidly. She soon smiled at her old friend and said, "Good thing I had you with me!"

Karen smiled and said, "Let's get you some food to eat, OK?"

Mom nodded and took an energy bar and some chocolate from Karen. About halfway through, Karen noticed Mom's breathing was slowing down and seemed to be returning to normal.

For a moment the two were quiet on Wheat Island. The emergency had passed. Karen got up to get the last bits of water out of Mom's boat, but then from somewhere nearby, they both heard a loud massive gush of air that lasted several long seconds.

Mom and Karen paused, held their breath, and listened.

Another powerful burst of air came again, this time lasting longer, like a gigantic sigh.

Mom gaped at Karen with wide eyes. "Are we not the only mammals on this island?"

Karen replied, "I would say we are definitely not alone. Except I think the mammal we are hearing belongs in the water."

Stranded

A split second later, Mom and Karen jumped up. They quickly tracked the animal's long, loud, and labored breathing. It was easy to find the whale.

The two friends hiked over a tiny hill, and there it was. A large humpback lay stranded on a sand spit between some rocks. The whale was completely out of the water, breathing heavily and thrashing its tail.

"Poor thing," Mom muttered. "What do you think happened?"

"It's hard to tell," Karen replied. "But this part of Maine has huge swings in the tides—up to twelve feet, and sometimes even fourteen feet. And that whale doesn't appear fully grown. I'd guess it is a yearling, and this may be its first year away from its mom. It might be that it was trying to scoop up some herring in the shallow waters or shoals right here." Karen pointed to the cove next to the island.

"It could have overshot its push to scoop up fish, and in its zeal for a meal it thrust itself right onto the beach. Then the tide went out and, well, here it is now, high and dry."

Mom and Karen stared for a moment at the massive creature, watching it breathe and, at times, thrash about.

"Fully grown or not," Mom commented, "it sure is big."

"I'm only speculating on how it got here. Perhaps we'll never really know," Karen said. "But I am sure of what we need to do now."

Karen looked at Mom. "Are you OK? Completely recovered?"

"Oh, yeah," Mom replied nonchalantly. "I'm absolutely fine."

"OK then, come with me." Karen led Mom quickly back to the kayaks. There she stuffed buckets, water bottles, and her water pump into a bag and handed it all to Mom. Then she grabbed some more supplies to carry.

Karen retrieved her cell phone from her hatch, picked it up, and dialed. It rang twice before someone answered.

Karen spoke. "We have a presumed yearling humpback whale stranded on Wheat Island. It's alive and thrashing about. We are two kayakers, Karen Francoeur and Kristen Parker, who happened upon the island."

Karen listened then said, "OK, got it," and hung up the phone.

Mom asked, "What did they say?"

"Follow me," Karen replied.

As they hustled back to the whale, Karen told Mom what was going on. "They're assembling a crew and boat to come out. They think it will be one to two hours before they're here, though. In the meantime, they told us we can help by trying to keep the whale wet."

Mom and Karen arrived back at the whale. Karen held Mom's arm for a moment. "Whatever you do, don't get anywhere near the flippers or tail. You've seen it thrashing around. We could easily get hurt trying to help the whale. Also, we have to make sure water doesn't get into the blowhole. That's like getting water up your nose. So, we're going to use these water bottles, and if I can get enough distance, I'll pump water from the ocean right onto the whale. We'll keep doing that until help arrives."

Meanwhile, the rest of the Parkers and the other passengers on the mail boat ferry had just docked at Stonington. They were climbing off the boat with their gear in hand when they heard an announcement coming off the boat's marine band radio: "Sécurité, sécurité, sécurité. Marine Mammal Stranding Hotline. We've got a report of a stranded humpback whale on Wheat Island. Report was given by two female kayakers. One is

There are three general calls a marine vessel can make to alert others. "Securité" sends out a general message about weather, safety, navigation, or an unusual situation. "Pan-pan" is more urgent but isn't for a grave or imminent threat. Mechanical breakdowns often get a "pan-pan" call out. "Mayday" is only used when the vessel and/or people on board are in immediate, grave danger.

a local outfitter. A marine mammal rescue center has been contacted and they are sending out a crew."

Morgan, James, Dad, and Ann, Karen's friend, all looked at each other. "That's Mom and Karen out there!" Morgan exclaimed.

The four held still for a moment. Then Dad said, "Let's quickly get our gear back in the car."

The car was parked on the pier, just a few feet away. Once their gear was stowed, Dad said, "Come on. Let's see what else we can find out."

Ann was still at the dock when Morgan, James, and Dad ran up. "I just tried to call Karen, but there was no answer," Ann reported. "I have to go, but I'll keep trying to check in with Karen to keep up with what's going on." Ann handed Dad a business card with Karen's number written on the back. "You can call me if you don't get any more information." She wished the family, and the whale, good luck.

Dad hurried the twins back to the ticket window for the mail boat and said, "Excuse me. Can I ask you a question?"

Dad told the woman at the ticket office that his wife and friend were the ones on the island with the whale. Then he asked, "Is there any way my kids and I can get out there?"

The woman pointed to a man off to the side. "Randy is heading out to watch and try to assist. You might see if there's room on his boat."

• • •

While Karen pumped water from the ocean to spray the whale, Mom filled buckets to douse it. They both worked furiously.

At one point Mom paused to wipe sweat off her forehead. She was not more than a few feet from the whale's eye. Something drew her in, and she paused and stared at the massive mammal. The whale's sides heaved in and out with each long, drawn-out, labored breath.

Mom was led to speak to the whale. "Hold on," she said. "We're doing the best we can, and help is coming soon."

Mom spontaneously reached over and stroked the whale, just above its eye. She knew it was dangerous to get so close, but her compassion for the whale and its plight made her forget for a second her own safety.

The whale seemed to respond by closing the eye and opening it again.

Mom smiled. "Am I imaging things, or did you just blink at me?"

The whale opened and closed its eye again.

"All right, Blinkie," Mom responded, giving the whale a name.

Right about then, the first boat arrived. It was a lobster boat and the crew on board anchored down in the water and took a small raft to the island. In an instant there were six people keeping Blinkie wet.

Shortly, tiny Wheat Island in the Gulf of Maine became a metropolis of people helping the whale. Some anchored at sea and took smaller craft in. Others observed the goings-on as best they could from their boats.

Then an Allied Whale boat arrived, carrying a marine mammal rescue crew. Once on the island, their leader quickly assessed the situation. She also asked Karen and Mom some questions.

Mom and Karen gave all the information they could. And Mom added, "We're calling the whale Blinkie, at least for now."

"Blinkie it is," the Allied Whale person responded.

The woman in charge introduced herself. "I'm Rosie of Allied Whale and the College of the Atlantic." Rosie looked around at all the people helping out on the island. "It's quite a crowd out here."

Then Rosie said, "I'm really not sure there is much else we should do at this point other than what we are doing, and wait. Being patient is doing something. The tide is returning, and that probably is our best course of action to try and save the whale. If we attempt to hoist and move it, we could hurt it, and we don't have equipment here for that now anyway."

Rosie snapped several photos of the whale, paying particular attention to the tail fluke. She explained, "These photos, hopefully, will help us identify the whale later."

Mom asked, worried, "But it needs to be in the water, right?"

"Absolutely," Rosie replied. "If it stays out too long, it can get severely sunburned." Rosie looked at all the people keeping the whale moist. "But it also needs to be in the water because its insides can get crushed being on land."

Karen grabbed Mom's arm. "Look!"

Water from a wave was lapping up to and around Blinkie's fluke. The whale then thrust down its tail, splashing up a spray of water.

"The tide is returning!" Mom exclaimed.

Rosie added, "In a few hours, hopefully, our whale could be back at sea, naturally. And that's the best thing."

Right then three familiar faces ran up to Kristen. "Hi, Mom!" Morgan said, hugging her.

"Hey—great to see you!" Mom said to the twins and her husband. "How did you get out here?"

"We hitched a ride with a lobster boat," Dad replied, pointing to one of the many boats anchored nearby.

"Well, welcome to Wheat Island!" Mom said. She pointed to the reason everyone was there. "Let's not stand here, let's help Blinkie stay wet!"

"Blinkie?!" James said as he, Morgan, and Dad also began dumping bottles of water on the whale.

"I'll tell you later," Mom said as she ran for more water.

The Parkers and all the others now on the island worked diligently to keep Blinkie wet. And, as the whale was continually showered with water and attention, it seemed to respond. Blinkie thrashed her tail more often and at times tried to move her body around in the moist sand.

Suddenly a larger wave washed up onto the small beach. Water sloshed and swirled around Blinkie and many of the people helping out.

The sudden rush of ocean gave Blinkie a fleeting moment of buoyancy. The whale rolled around before the water sucked back to sea, then she settled again on the sand, still stranded.

More waves rolled in, and the water level rose quickly. Morgan, James, Mom, and Dad, though, continued to pour water onto various dry areas on the whale.

Eventually, after a larger swell circulated all the way around Blinkie, Rosie from Allied Whale stood on a rock, cupped her hands, and shouted, "It's time for everyone to stand back! The tide's well on its way and Blinkie . . ." Rosie paused for a second, realizing she just formally introduced everyone to the whale. "Blinkie may be able to free itself with any one of these incoming waves and the higher tide."

"Please, for the whale's sake and everyone's safety," Rosie continued, "stay back from Blinkie now!"

The Parkers and everyone else on Wheat Island climbed to high ground, a mere five or so feet above sea level. But that kept them away from the whale and the incoming tide.

Waves continued to roll in, some spilling onto the beach higher than others. James said after a fairly large wave flowed again all around the whale, "C'mon, Blinkie, hang in there. The tide is returning and you should be in the ocean soon."

The largest wave yet poured in and circulated around the whale, lifting it again off the sand. Blinkie responded by thrashing about and moving this time several feet.

Morgan called out, "You can do it, Blinkie! You can free yourself!"

With each passing surge of tide, water now was free-flowing around the whale, remaining there even as the waves sucked back out. The large whale reacted by thrashing around more and more. Then everyone on Wheat Island began cheering on Blinkie.

Finally it happened. A large swell engulfed the beach Blinkie was on, pouring water on, around, and even briefly over parts of the whale.

Blinkie was instantly lifted and this time surged off the beach and into the ocean. The humpback immediately swam out to sea, toward deeper water.

Everyone on the island celebrated with cheers, high fives, and clapping. Morgan called out, "Way to go, Blinkie! You did it—you're free!"

When Blinkie was a good distance out, the whale thrust itself above the water's surface with a grand, leaping, twisting breach, then splashed back into the ocean.

The Parkers looked at each other, astonished at what they saw.

Then Blinkie did it again. And again. And again. She breached at least a dozen times, each leap seemingly higher and more graceful than the last and with twists and turns in the whale's splash back down to sea.

Mom smiled and said, "That is one happy whale."

Soon, everyone began leaving Wheat Island. Most took craft to their larger boats nearby. But Mom and Karen, despite being offered rides, decided to finish what they started and paddle into Stonington by kayak.

After pumping the remaining water out of her boat, Mom hugged her family good-bye again and she and Karen took off to sea. Morgan, James, and Dad had to wait a while for boat traffic in the area to ease before they got back on their lobster boat and began heading to the mainland.

• • •

Mom and Karen crossed a large expanse of water called Merchant Row. Karen plotted a course on her chart, checking the compass on her kayak's deck to assure safe crossing. They paddled along the shore of McGlathery Island. The beautiful rocky island and calm waters near shore led Mom to say, "You sure have a lot to see here in the Gulf of Maine."

Karen smiled, "We are very lucky."

As soon as they passed along Bear Island, Karen pointed out more birds. "Those over there are eiders," she said. "Their soft feathers are the ones used for down pillows and sleeping bags."

After passing the Potato Islands, they were nearly to Stonington and could see the harbor straight ahead. Mom broke into song.

> Down by the bay
> Where the watermelons grow
> Back to my home
> I dare not go
> For if I do
> My mother would say
> "Have you ever seen a whale with a polka dot tail?"
> Down by the bay

Karen joined Mom for the second verse.

> Down by the bay
> Where the watermelons grow
> Back to my home
> I dare not go
> For if I do
> My mother would say
> "Have you ever seen an eider eating a spider?"
> Down by the bay

And just as Mom and Karen were about to churn up a third stanza of "Down by the Bay," a boat chugging by caught their attention. Mom looked over and saw the lobster boat. Three very recognizable passengers waved to her. Mom smiled and waved back.

"I wonder what took them so long to get here," Mom said.

"Traffic getting out of Wheat Island," Karen responded. "Let's just say it was an Acadia version of rush hour."

Then James shouted, "Keep singing!"

Mom and Karen did so, and the Parkers on the boat joined in.

Down by the bay
Where the watermelons grow
Back to my home
I dare not go
For if I do
My mother would say
"Have you ever seen a puffin eating a muffin?"
Down by the bay!

Moments later both the lobster boat and Mom and Karen reached
the shore. Morgan, James, and Dad came over to Mom and helped carry
the kayaks to Karen's car and load and tie them to the roof. Then Mom
hugged Karen. "Let's not let another twenty years go by, OK?"

"Absolutely not."

And with that, the Parkers drove back to Bar Harbor and Blackwoods Campground for one more night in Acadia.

The First Shall Be the Last

"Bye, Mom, see you at the top!" James said as he, Dad, and Morgan exited the car at the trailhead near Blackwoods Campground.

It was 4:30 a.m. and not even light out.

"We better get going," Dad said, "or else we'll miss the show."

Mom took off driving for the summit of Cadillac Mountain. But Morgan, James, and Dad were hiking up.

The first part of the trail climbed through a rocky, rooty section of the forest. Morgan, James, and Dad had on headlamps but, slowly, daylight began to emerge, and as their eyes adjusted, the lights eventually were no longer needed.

Just past a mile in, Dad and the twins took the short spur trail to Eagles Crag. They left the forest and hiked along rock outcrops. Dad checked the time again. "5:05," he announced. "This should be our moment."

Right about then, Mom arrived at the 1,530-foot summit, Acadia's tallest peak. "It's crowded," Mom said to herself, noticing all the cars in the parking lot and people scrambling urgently to the rocks nearby to get a view. "I guess this really is a big deal!"

Mom jumped out of the car and joined the others in and around the short Summit Loop Trail. Everyone gazed east at the steadily but ever-so-slowly brightening sky. It was 5:14 a.m.

THE FIRST TO SEE THE SUN?!

At 1,530 feet, Cadillac Mountain is Acadia's highest peak and the tallest mountain along the North Atlantic Seaboard. Cadillac Mountain is also the first place to see the sunrise in the continental United States from October 7 until March 6. In the summer it is *one of* the first places, challenged by an island slightly farther east, but that area is often foggy, making Cadillac the *best place* to see the first of the sun.

"One more minute!" someone called out.

Mom and what seemed like hundreds of others watched where the colors of the sky indicated that the sun was going to appear. Someone in the crowd started counting down, and many others joined in.

"10, 9, 8, 7, 6, 5, 4, 3, 2, 1 . . . Sunrise!" everyone shouted. And there it was, the sun slowly peeking over the horizon, beginning a new day.

"The first to see it," Mom said to herself.

A few seconds later, Morgan, James, and Dad also watched the sun come up and light up Mount Desert Island and Acadia as well as the nearby Atlantic Ocean and coastal islands.

Dad took on the deep voice of a sports announcer. He cupped his hands around his mouth and said, "There it is, everyone. The first place in the continental United States to see the sunrise!"

Morgan and James cheered, "Whoo-hoo!"

"But Mom saw it first," Morgan said.

"Barely," James added.

"It probably was pretty much exactly the same," Dad said while glancing at his watch. It was now 5:18, and the sun was fully above the ocean. "Well, either way, welcome to a new day, kids. It's a brand-new day!"

Morgan, James, and Dad headed toward the summit, about three miles away. As the trail climbed steadily, every once in a while one of them would turn around. "The views just keep getting better and better," Dad said while gazing toward the Atlantic and some of Bar Harbor's nearby offshore islands.

Now that the sunrise was over, the early-morning hikers slowed down noticeably. James said about their more-casual pace, "Why should we hurry? It's our last hike and summit climb in Acadia."

"I totally agree," Dad said.

Morgan noticed along the trail what they had been enjoying all week in the park, and one of Maine's most famous delicacies. "Blueberries!" she announced. Morgan, James, and Dad picked and ate some, then walked on only to quickly find more, again and again.

Dad saved some of the tasty treats in a baggie for Mom. "I'm going to miss these," he commented.

Soon they came to a wooden bench overlooking Featherbed Pond. They sat down, pulled out some snacks, and looked over the marshy, calm body of water.

"What a nice little surprise," Dad said.

Dpppp . . . Dpp . . . Dp.

Morgan, James, and Dad looked at each other. "It's a green frog!" James said, recalling the ranger's "Sounds of Acadia" talk the night before.

The Parkers sat quietly, listening and watching the pond.

Dpp.

"There it is again," Morgan whispered.

"I wonder where the frog is," James added.

Dpp.

"Boy, that ranger sure nailed what a green frog sounds like," Dad said.

"Maybe it wasn't the ranger imitating the frog, but the frog is now imitating the ranger," James said, then laughed at his joke.

Dad glanced toward the summit, then at his watch. "It's almost seven o'clock," he announced. "C'mon, Mom is expecting us."

The three Parkers hiked on. The trail continued to climb, now mostly over rocky areas, with the distinctive, Bates-style cairns marking the path.

Soon they could make out people on the summit and the sound of cars driving up the road. Near the top there was one iron rung placed on a rock to help hikers over.

"That's a little token one for our memory's sake," Dad said.

Finally they reached the top of the mountain. Morgan, James, and Dad approached the parking area and crossed over to the Summit Loop Trail.

"Boy, it's crowded up here," Dad said, noticing all the people milling about.

"The ranger said that five thousand people a day come up here," Morgan mentioned. "And that Acadia last year was the ninth most visited national park in the country."

"There's one of Acadia's best visitors over there," Dad said while waving to Mom.

Mom waved back and walked down to greet her family. "Well, how was it?"

"Phenomenal," Dad replied. "Couldn't have been better. And how about up here?"

"The same," Mom answered. "I made a nice sketch of Cadillac Mountain with the ocean and islands in the distance."

Morgan, James, Mom, and Dad shared their sunrise details, then all four Parkers walked over to the posted displays, noticing landmarks visible from the top of the mountain.

"There's Blackwoods Campground," Morgan pointed out.

"And Egg Island," James said. "Hello crabs, lobsters, and blood stars," he said to Diver Ed's sea creatures.

"There's Little Cranberry Island," Mom gestured while looking at Morgan.

"And the Bubbles near Jordan Pond," Dad said, looking the other direction. "You can see just about everything up here!"

While the family gazed at Acadia, missing it already before even leaving, Morgan pulled out her journal and wrote.

Dear Diary:

I am so sad to leave Acadia. This is such a unique place. As Mom says, "It is like no national park we have ever been to before." I think, maybe next summer, we plan to spend a whole month here. There's much more kayaking, hiking, and ranger programs to do—that's for sure. I know we will be on the Precipice and Beehive trails again, too! Here is my top ten list for Acadia:

1. Peregrine Watch at Echo Lake
2. Cadillac Mountain sunrise
3. The Wonderland Trail
4. Isle au Haut and camping in our shelter
5. Precipice Trail, ladders and all
6. Beehive Trail, iron rungs and all
7. Thunder Hole
8. Sand Beach and Echo Lake swimming!
9. The carriage roads by bike
10. Bubble Pond

I am going to miss you, Acadia!

Au revoir,

Morgan

And James wrote this:

This is James Parker reporting:

Acadia is the BEST! I could hike on the trails here forever. As we all have said, "They're addictive and adventurous—like being on Tom Sawyer's Island at Disneyland." My top ten list will be about the trails and the great ranger programs. I don't know which I liked the best:

1. Diver Ed, Mini-Ed, and the bag of sea creatures
2. Tide pools at Tidepool School
3. Super Sand Sleuths at Sand Beach
4. The Beehive
5. The Homans and Emery Loop Trail
6. Jordan Cliffs Trail
7. Bubble Rock
8. Duck Harbor Mountain
9. The rescued whale on Wheat Island
10. Popovers and Bar Harbor Bars at the Jordan Pond House and store

Good-bye, Acadia—I'll see you again soon, I promise.

James Parker

The family stood at the summit, transfixed at the views and trying to soak in their final moments.

Dad eventually glanced at his watch. "Whoa!" he exclaimed. "We could have ended up staying here until sunset!"

"But we do have a plane to catch," Mom reminded her family. She put her arms around the twins and escorted them to the car. "I hate saying good-bye," Mom admitted. "But I guess we have to, at least for now . . ."

The Adoption

Back home on the West Coast, Morgan, James, and their parents often wondered about Blinkie. One day at breakfast, a month after their return, they were talking about the whale.

"Do you think Allied Whale kept the name we gave it?" James asked.

"From what I understand," Mom answered, "they like to give it a name that would help identify or pick out a marking on its tail."

Dad turned on the computer. "I'm going to e-mail them to see if they have seen Blinkie at all anywhere." Dad drafted a short letter about Blinkie, reminding Allied Whale that they were some of the people involved in helping save the yearling humpback.

A few hours later, the Parkers had their answer. It was a response from Rosie and it read:

> Dear Morgan, James, Kristen, and Robert: It is great to hear from you! As you may know, many times beached whales do not end up with a happy ending. They are beached for different reasons. But your whale, "Blinkie," we believe accidently got onto the sand going after fish and was stuck there at low tide. I also think Kristen and Karen's quick response could be a major reason that Blinkie is now OK!

We took pictures of Blinkie's tail fluke, and there are some clear patterns or markings on the tail that make Blinkie easy to identify if it is seen and photographed again.

And I am so happy to say Blinkie has been observed by several boats out near Isle au Haut, cruising along, with an occasional breach thrown in. It was definitely Blinkie, so our whale is alive and well, thanks to you and many others!

Sincerely,
Rosie
Allied Whale

PS—Did you know we have an adopt-a-whale program? If you choose to become a part of this, your contribution will help fund the largest whale photo identification program in the world. You'll also get pictures of your whale, Blinkie's bio, which you are already very familiar with, and her complete sighting history. You'll get a booklet on whale adoption and a bumper sticker, too.

Think about it, but whatever you do, please stay in touch!

The Parkers closed the e-mail from Rosie and looked at each other, answering without saying a word.

Finally Mom said, "I'm signing us up right now!"